ZHOU YAPING

IF THE WH
DIES

如果麦子死了

周亚平 著

郑秀才
Jeffrey Twitchell-Waas
Paul Manfredi
译

江苏凤凰文艺出版社
JIANGSU PHOENIX LITERATURE AND ART PUBLISHING

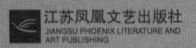

EAT

CONTENTS

Translated by

Suzanne Zheng
Jeffrey Twitchell-Waas
Paul Manfredi

If the Wheat Dies

001　**Introduction**

Paper Puppets

012　Paper Puppets　　纸偶
013　If the Wheat Dies　　如果麦子死了
014　The Brilliant Prerequisite　　灿烂的前提
015　Love Had Better Start Early　　恋爱还是要及早开始
016　Silversmith Shop　　银匠铺子
017　Dog Basket　　狗筐
018　Grey Dog　　灰狗
020　We'll Mess Things Up　　我们会把东西弄坏
022　Cog　　嵌齿
024　The Crow Won't Be Regarded as Divine　　乌鸦不会被视为神明
026　Commemoration 2　　纪念 2
028　Commemoration 3　　纪念 3
029　Prayer　　祈祷
030　Extravagant Illumination　　奢侈的照明
032　Secret Garden　　秘密花园
034　It's Just That, at Center Stage, Slowly, Black Waters Gather　　只是，舞场中央慢慢积聚起黑色的水
036　The Cartoon Deemed Ridiculous from the Start　　卡通一开始就被定义为荒谬
037　Involvement with Sweet Death　　与甜蜜死亡的干系
038　We Are Playing Games Barefoot　　我们赤着脚在做游戏
040　Waves Surprisingly Surge from Underneath　　它的下面竟泛出波涛

I

042	You Put Yourself In	你把自己放了进去
044	Sincerity in the River's Morning Water	赤诚在早间的河水
046	Hallucination	幻象
048	This Rock Would Like to Flower	这块石头想开花
050	Jump, Jump, Jump, Jump!	跳，跳，跳，跳！
051	Kneeling or Crouching Sex	跪着或趴下
052	A Poem Changes Direction While Writing	一首诗在写作中改变了方向
054	This Rotten Poem Is for Pound	把这首烂诗送给庞德
056	Tense Relations	紧张关系
060	Love in Despair	绝望爱情
064	Offer Modigliani a Subject	送莫迪里阿尼一个题材
068	The Height of the Master Almost Reaches the Eaves	大师的身高已快接近房檐
069	The Mortality of Happiness Is Twice That of Loneliness	快乐死亡率高于孤独一倍
070	Counteraction	反制
072	All Protection Lost	所有的庇护都在丧失
074	Misappropriation, My Scheme	挪用，我的预谋
076	Tattoo	刺青
078	Connection	联系
080	Predicament	困境
082	Blood-colored Jam	血色之果酱
084	Love in the Last Glow of Sunset	爱在落日余晖
086	Enter You, Just As Anxiety Finds a Wonderful Dream	进入你，就像焦虑找到了美梦
088	To Sarah Kane	致萨拉·凯恩
089	Reaction	反应

090	To Godard	致戈达尔
092	Border: To Bei Dao	边界：致北岛
094	Bright Reality	明亮的现实
096	Vivacious Body	昂扬的身体
098	Eavesdropping on the Soul	偷听灵魂
099	Fragile	脆弱
100	Irrigation Is the Lifeblood of Agriculture	水利是农业的命脉
102	Lowly	卑微
104	Grace	恩泽
106	Snow Piled Up on the Mountains	白雪已积满群山
108	Part-timer Chicks Come Here in Spring	打工的小鸟春天来
109	Red Memory	红的记忆
110	A Crane Rests on the Roof	仙鹤歇在房顶
112	To Kerouac	致凯鲁亚克
114	Zidane	齐内
116	Yoko Ono	小野洋子
117	The Flame's Distortion	火焰的篡改
118	A Narrow Staircase	一架窄梯
120	Neither Bright Nor Upright	不光明正大
122	This Is the Biggest Horse I Saw Today	这是今天看到的最大的马
124	Airport Railway Express	机场快轨
126	I Need Something Dry	我需要一些干燥的东西
128	The Green Monster	绿怪兽
130	Going Up to Yunnan	上云南
132	Jaipur	斋浦尔
134	Paris	巴黎
135	Goddess	神

136	I've Slept with the Sea	我睡过大海
140	Decorating Ourselves as Tanks, We Wouldn't Look for Love	把自己包装成坦克一样，就不打算恋爱了
142	Meaning and Horse	语义和马
144	Grammar	语法
145	Silent Fantasy	平静的异想
146	Different from Trains that I Saw	和我见到的列车不一样
147	Untitled	无题
148	Copulating Ants	交媾的蚂蚁
150	Joyful Things	欢乐的事情
152	Feeding	喂食
154	The Play at the Kaiming Theatre	开明剧场的戏剧
156	Passing Rain-Flower Terrace	经过雨花台
158	Imitate Classical Philosophy	仿古典哲学
159	Fake Aphorism	伪格言
160	Greedy Sheep	贪婪的羊
162	Our Country's Agriculture	我国农业
164	Ride a Jet	乘坐喷气式飞机
168	Fresh Wood	新鲜的木材
170	Behavioral Error	行为的过失

Magicicada

200	Oh, My Heart of Hearts	哦，内心
202	Irony	反讽
206	The Parakeet by Water	水边鹦鹉
220	The Avant-Garde	先锋派
226	By Rice Straws	稻草旁
230	White Sand Spring 1	白沙泉 1
232	White Sand Spring 2	白沙泉 2
234	Maize (Jade Rice) Master	玉米师傅
258	I'll Write about Autumn Dusk in the Mountains	我将写山居秋暝
266	Control	支配
270	For Joe Hisaishi	致久石让
272	One is Still in Sweden, The Other One is Already in Norway	一个还在瑞典，一个已到挪威
278	Passing Through These Things, Enough Movement	通过这些事物，足够地移动

NTRODUCTION

In China, Zhou Yaping 周亚平 (1961-) is a familiar name as an executive television producer for China's major television network, China Central Television (CCTV). Yet beneath this official persona, lives a very different face, Zhou Yaping the poet. Despite his success in popular media, Zhou's first love has always been poetry, to which he has devoted considerable energy since 1983. During his formative period, he remained a relatively marginal figure in the Chinese literary scene, dismissing acceptance and popularity as mediocrity. Zhou even gave up creative writing after 1994 out of a sense of national malaise. After a 15-year hiatus, however, he returned to poetry in 2008 with renewed energy and remarkable productivity. In less than two years, he published three books of poems, followed in 2013 by his collected poems, *Red White Blue Grey Black Black* (红白蓝灰黑黑) and a selection, *Original* (原样). Since then, Zhou Yaping *Original* has one or two new collections coming out each year (See the details in the attached Bibliography).

Zhou Yaping's professional and literary evolutions have been intertwining, while at the same time distinct. Zhou graduated from a police college in 1983, where he then took up a position as an instructor of politics for the next decade. At the same time, he was attending the Writer's Class at Nanjing University. Together with his roommate Che Qianzi (车前子), he established a poetry group called the Formalists (形式主义派), which brought out a self-published magazine entitled 《 原样 》 (*Original*) that contains both their own poems and statements on poetics. Zhou Yaping took a leading role in the critical articulation of a formalist poetics that stressed the presentation of forms and images rather than the expression of emotions and ideas. As a writer, Zhou is playful, though he takes the game of writing very seriously. He and Che would often engage in inspired, if somewhat erratic, behavior, suddenly leaping up to paint their ceiling in various colors and with strange symbols, for instance, before just as precipitously returning to their desks to continue writing poems. Fragments of these experiences occasionally emerge in his poetry, but more importantly formed the playful and experimental mindset evident in the poetry composed early in his career. Zhou's most experimental poems written in the late1980s and early 1990s, such as "Art, 69 Chapters" (艺六十九章) and "The Master of Maize" (玉米师傅) were incomprehensible to contemporary Chinese critics whose understanding was limited by conventional poetic assumptions.

If few readers at that time could appreciate his efforts as a pioneering poet, he did receive some positive appraisal from outside China. In particular the British poet, J. H. Prynne, who met Zhou Yaping and Che Qianzi in Suzhou in 1991, has brought these poets to attention within the context of radical poetries in English, sponsoring the translation of a group anthology, *Original: Chinese Language-Poetry Group* (1994), which included his important afterword. Although it remains common in the literature field to regard him as a representative of Chinese language poetry, Zhou claims that this appellation was a banner given by critics and translators who found superficial similarities between their work and so-called language poetries in English. His poetics, in fact, is better summarized by the appellation "formalism," which he and Che Qianzi used for their original group. In essence, they strove to depict the "original forms" of things as they are. Zhou emphasized this point on the back cover of his recent collection *Original*: "I don't believe that I have composed another shape for the world."

Zhou Yaping's interest in forms and images can be attributed in part to his background in painting and design. During his middle school years, he studied painting with a teacher who had been sent down from college to design bed sheets in a local factory. At that early age, besides painting techniques, Zhou also learned by heart sheet design patterns, including the rules for two-directional and four-directional continuities in pattern-making. Similarly, images in Zhou's poetry are often the language units themselves combined according to similarity, variation and contrasts. This is why many of his poems, especially long ones, have a tendency to read like collage. From a series of images a perceptive reader can create a suggestion of narrative. Zhou's imagist tendencies also lead him to publicly reject the use of analogy (比喻), whether conceived of as simile or metaphor, which he regards as a low technique. Zhou Yaping's images are not decoratively added to the flow of words to modify content; instead, they are the content and the formal components of the poem.

After leaving the police college in 1994, Zhou began working with Suzhou Television, and eventually joined major media institutions in Beijing, first the Central Newsreel and Documentary Film Studio and then CCTV. His accomplishments in public media were initially as a documentary director, making many cultural and historical films, including two official works for the 2010 World Expo in Shanghai. At CCTV, Zhou has held a leading position in the television administration and played a key role in deciding what stories Chinese would watch on the CCTV channels. Zhou Yaping strove to move the Chinese television industry beyond the confines of ideological discourse and authoritarianism, to become more market oriented and geared to international practice. No other poet can compare with Zhou Yaping's influence on the Chinese entertainment industry. But in 2015, his reformative effort was called to a stop and he withdrew from CCTV. He put more effort into film production, worked as Art Director for his son, the young director Zhou Kan, and helped him finish writing and directing three drama films. In 2016, Zhou Yaping made a short art film, "When the Film Is Poems," which features his own poems.

Although he dismisses the appellation of "language poetry," Zhou Yaping still put crucial importance on language in his poetics. In a recent interview with poet Chen Mo (陈陌), Zhou remarks that: "Poetry, in my opinion, is an art that draws the shape of the language." He later explained that: "The world is language. Every form of art is an art of language, but poetry is about words, it completes the language with words." The view that the world is determined by language is not unfamiliar among poets and poetry critics. In T. E. Hulme's opinion, language is the gossamer web woven between actual things, through which people see the world. Those parts which are not mentioned in language are overlooked. With the creation of new phrases or syntactic patterns, poets modify and complement this gossamer web, changing what are looked at and seen through the web. The contemporary Chinese poet Yu Jian (于坚) also held similar ideas: "Language explains the world. It provides meanings for existence and also conceptualizes the world…Poetry is the emancipation of language and its incessant pursuit of liberty. This is the original calling of poetry."

Compared with his early writing, Zhou Yaping's recent poetry refers more freely to contemporary phenomena, mundane objects and even his own body, so freely that they might be considered as adhering to Yu Jian's claim that "The Dao exists even in feces and urine." Zhou does not avoid the dirty and strange as would a more "comfortable" aesthetics. On the other hand, in his poetry, objects are frequently bundled in literary tropes, such as metaphor, synecdoche, metonymy and allegory. Although, the same as Yu Jian, Zhou Yaping resists defining the poetic in terms of rhetoric effect, this does not mean that his poems avoid use of literary tropes. The literary effect of tropes is not the aim of his writing or its structuring rule, rather the tropes are simply compositional elements that serve his purpose of describing the world. Literary tropes are used to displace fixed and habitual relationships in proper naming of ordinary language. Sometimes the figurative phrases are unconventional synecdochic signs in a naturalistic narrative; sometimes they are closer to allegorical symbols, the narrative of which manifests the essence of a category of things. Zhou Yaping's figurative language often seems like strange combinations of words and objects, whose ultimate meanings are ambiguous. But by using unconventional signifiers, Zhou Yaping catches "insignificant" details or alternative perspectives on objects, which are lost in ordinary language. Our view of the world can be changed by looking at it through the lens of his creative description.

Even when using plain language to reach the world, Zhou prefers to display dramatic contrasts and the defamiliarizing strangeness in daily life, bringing out the poetic in ordinary objects. Typical poetic figures from the romantic tradition, such as the moon, light, cloud, may also appear in his poems and still shine their traditional idealistic glamour. But Zhou Yaping often deploys them unconventionally in very mundane contexts, resulting in burlesque caricatures from the point of view of idealistic aesthetics; however, in a sense, he also brings new life to them in the contemporary world.

Similar to Yu Jian, Zhou Yaping takes as his goal the objective description of contemporary life, but his approach is quite different. Yu Jian's poems tend to appear highly realistic with readily-recognizable settings and a respect to general syntax. In contrast, Zhou Yaping's vocabulary and syntax are completely his own. His references of things transcend general logic and ordinary language; his descriptions are flashing sparks ignited in the merge of his sensitive perception and insightful observation of things. He is also adept at representing the intangible with tangible images. He depicts the abstract forms of the world's phenomena from a perspective beyond our ordinary habitual perception. But Zhou says that he never uses his pen to doodle, he always writes down something that appears in front of his eyes. An image is therefore not created in the process of writing; he lives with an image before he writes it down. The prior existence of the charged images as such is the true meaning of his objective writing.

Yu Jian insists that the vocation of poets is to represent the abstract truth of the world, the "Heavenly Dao," and, at the same time, recover an "existential language" distinct from the tendency to use language as a mere practical tool. Indeed, no other Chinese poet from the same generation has achieved such a double goal of poetry writing as fully as Zhou Yaping does.

Zhou Yaping is a self-conscious avant-garde writer who challenges even readers predisposed to favor his early styles. He experiments restlessly, pursuing aesthetic satisfaction through innovative literary forms and modes of presentation rather than through the expression of mere content and emotion. His disjointed syntax, startling imagery and neologisms take aim at all manner of preconceptions, including those of his own style. He is pessimistic about the state of poetry moving forward, while at the same time a prolific writer and an active promoter of poetry. In his interview with Chen Mo, Zhou commented: "What I write has become an isolated island. I devote my entire effort to building and preserving this isolate island."

From a reader's perspective, the value of a poet is not measured by his recognition and fame. Instead, it is in his capacity of reaching into human experience, discovering, and then opening those tiny doors of its existence that we ourselves were unaware. We believe Zhou Yaping has such capacity. Our mission is similar to those who look for extra-terrestirals, sending messages from this planet to outer space and seeking a response from other intelligent beings. Although it seems naïve to believe in this hopeless search, we won't stop sending out our signals from this lonely world of poetry and waiting for resonance and response.

Bibliography

If the Wheat Dies (如果麦子死了 , Nanjing: Jiangsu Phoenix Literature and Art Publishing, 2009)
Vulgar Beauty (俗丽 , Nanjing: Jiangsu Phoenix Literature and Art Publishing, 2009)
Opera Theatre (戏剧场 , Nanjing: Jiangsu Phoenix Literature and Art Publishing, 2009)
Red White Blue Grey Black Black (红白蓝灰黑黑 , Nanjing: Jiangsu Phoenix Literature and Art Publishing, 2013)
Original (原样 , Wuhan: Changjiang Literature and Art Publishing House, 2013)
With the Public (在公众 , Nanjing: Jiangsu Phoenix Literature and Art Publishing, 2014)
The Crossed-Out Words (X 字 , Guangzhou: Flower City Press, 2015)
To the Sordid Taxi Driver (致龌龊司机 , Chongqing: Chongqing University Press, 2015).
A Supplement of To the Sordid Taxi Driver (补致龌龊司机删诗 , Beijing: Rubber Press, 2016)
Mr. Sun (日先生 , Beijing: One Villain and 49 Horses, 2017)
Short Movie: Magicicada (周期蝉 , 2017)

Parataxis: Modernism and Modern Writing that introduced these poets, Original: Chinese Language-Poetry Group (no.7, Fall 1994, Cambridge, UK)

Translators

Suzanne Zheng: Independent scholar in Bellevue, WA, U.S.A
Jeffrey Twitchell-Waas: Independent scholar in Switzerland
Paul Manfredi: Professor of Chinese at Pacific Lutheran University, Tacoma, WA, U.S.A

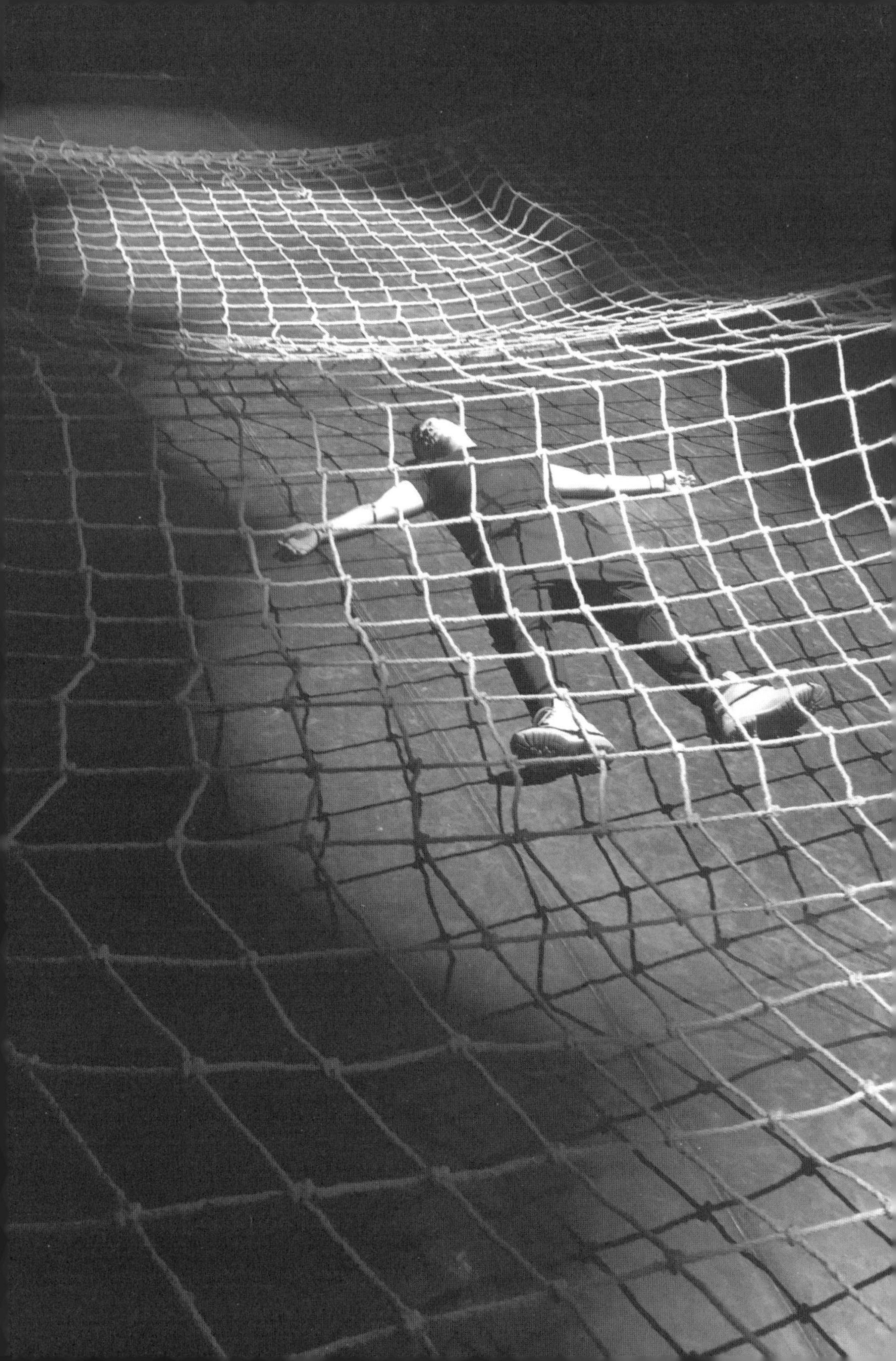

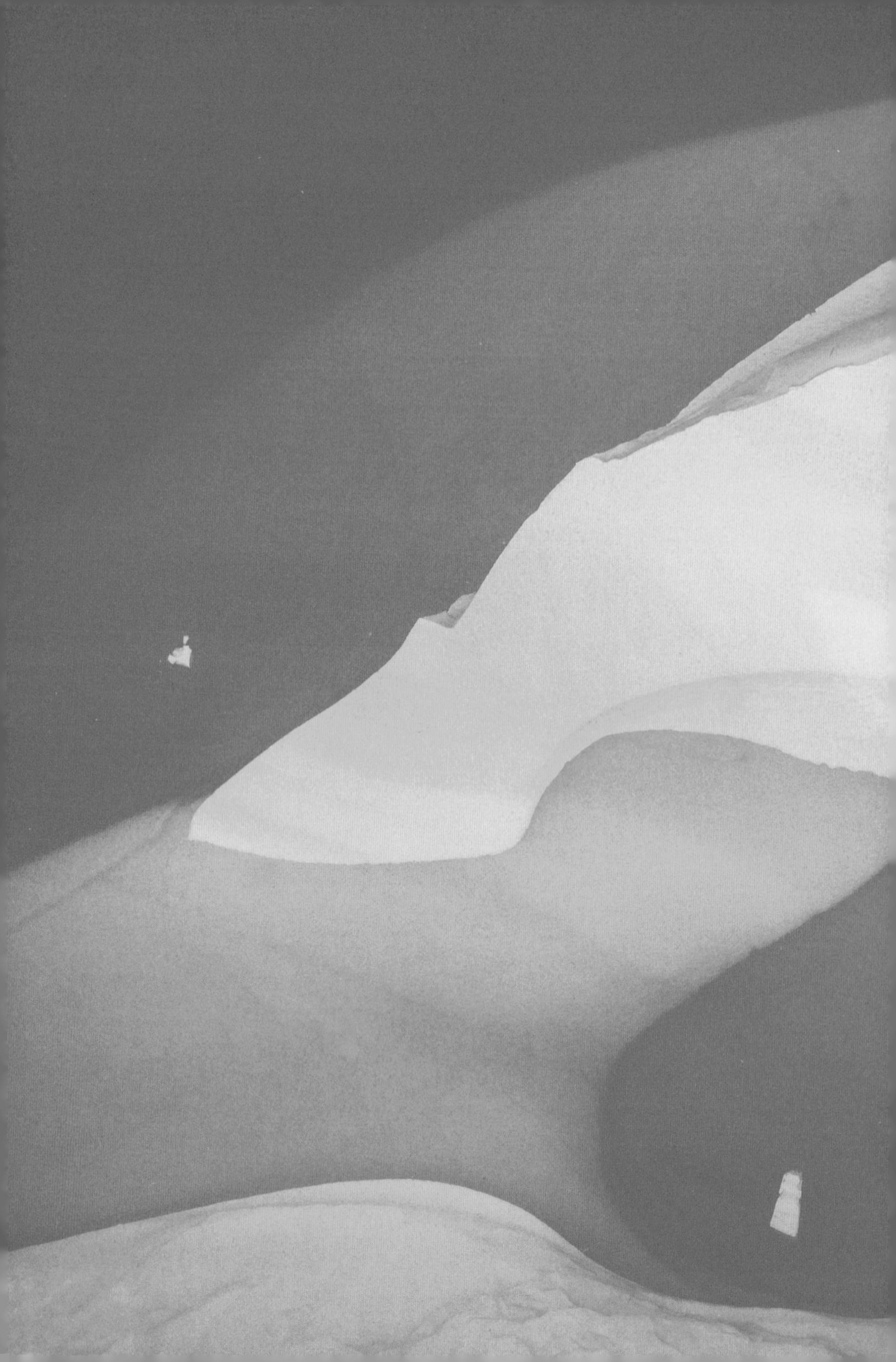

注：本诗集所刊图片部分取自电影《周期蝉》

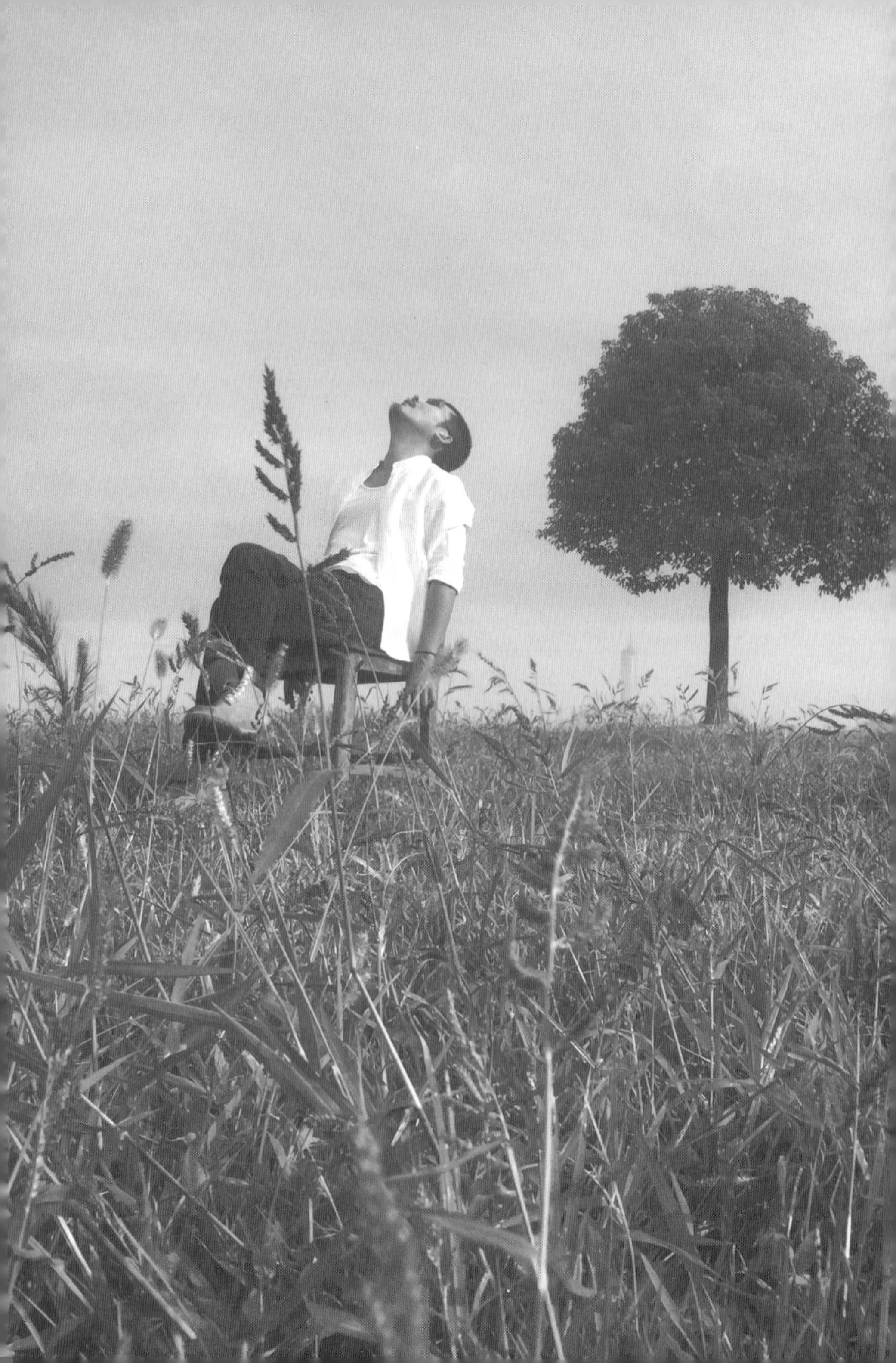

Paper Puppets

Translated by

Suzanne Zheng
Jeffrey Twitchell-Waas
Paul Manfredi

——

If the Wheat Dies

011

Paper Puppets

Make some paper puppets

let them farm in a golden pan

mother gives birth to us

only allowing us to cherish ourselves

纸偶

做一些纸偶

在金盘里种地

母亲生下我们

只让我们爱惜自己

If the Wheat Dies

If the wheat dies

the color of the land will turn scarlet,

if the wheat dies

the color of the land won't change until

next year's wheat comes up

如果麦子死了

如果麦子死了

地里的颜色会变得鲜红

如果麦子死了

要等到明年的麦子出来

才会改变地上的颜色

The Brilliant Prerequisite

Take a handful of grain and blow

hard. The kernel that takes flight

will lead us forward

灿烂的前提

将手中的一把麦粒

用力吹起。其中飞翔的一颗

它会带领我们走向前

Love Had Better Start Early

Love had better start early.

Peel off the stone's skin, layer by layer,

No dewdrop will be wrapped inside.

恋爱还是要及早开始

恋爱还是要及早开始。

剥开石头的皮，一层层，

里面不会裹着水珠。

Silversmith Shop

Hey Mister

make me a lock

for my wife

Gu Hongliu

银匠铺子

叫声师傅

打把锁

送给我的妻子

顾红柳

Dog Basket

The dog is the one and only on this strip of white line

the dog is the one and only on this patch of white snow

the dog is the one and only on this plot of white color

the dog, as you see it,

is the one and only bastard

狗筐

狗是这条白线上的唯一

狗是这块白雪上的唯一

狗是这块白色上的唯一

狗是你们眼中

唯一的狗东西

Grey Dog

He's already walked a long time

he's already walked a long way

out past Third Ring Road

beyond Fifth Ring Road

he yields to cars

as well as humanity

many people think he's lost

he's just looking for

a bitch of the same color

灰狗

它已走了很久

它已走了很远

走过三环

也走过五环

它避让汽车

也避让人类

许多人认为它是惘然的

它只在寻找

一条与它同样颜色的母狗

We'll Mess Things Up

Looking for a dark cloud

is a moment of peace for the wheat field

an early rising farmer rides a dark cloud

like a gentleman

wind follows the wheat wave

as for us, we'll just mess things up

我们会把东西弄坏

寻找乌云

是麦地宁静的时刻

早起的农民架乘乌云

也像绅士一样

风,跟随麦浪

而我们只会把东西弄坏

Cog

I wear a white top.

I wrap myself in a black scarf.

My two hands sunk deep into pockets.

I'm doing nothing.

But it's chaos all around.

The machine is broken.

In my palm, I also grasp a cog.

The right hand.

嵌齿

我穿着白色的上衣。

我裹着黑色的围巾。

我的双手插在口袋。

我什么也没干。

而周围一片混乱。

机器坏了。

我的手心也攥着一枚嵌齿。

右手。

The Crow Won't Be Regarded as Divine

We won't

designate the crow the national bird

but if possible, it'll

hang on the wall

sit straight in the living room

stand still in various solemn places

it'll be solid black

pure white

its songs will be sung

by great sons and daughters

乌鸦不会被视为神明

我们不会

把乌鸦定为国鸟

如果可能 它就会

挂在墙面

端坐客厅

伫立于各种庄严的地方

它会黑得坚强

白得纯洁

它的歌声都由

伟大的儿女演唱

Commemoration 2

I saw

human figures in the torch's flame

I saw chain

on the torch's base,

but it's not chaining

the black wave

the wave

is already tinged with the torch's

tears of

joy

纪念 2

我在

火炬中 看到了人形

我在火炬的根基中

看到了锁链

而它 并不锁住

黑色的潮流

潮流上

已经沾满火炬

欢乐的

眼泪

Commemoration 3

Cringing

winter birds,

the snow that you carry

is the tears of the birds

in heaven

纪念 3

畏缩着

冬天的小鸟

你们背驮的积雪

是天堂里

鸟儿的泪水

Prayer

You bend down

bullets pass over your head

祈祷

当你弯腰时

子弹穿过了你的头顶

Extravagant Illumination

Have burned the first part of the Divine Comedy

so we can go on

reading the rest

奢侈的照明

焚烧《神曲》的上部

我们才能将下部

读下去

Secret Garden

I live with a herd of animals

only I am dressed neat and tidy.

They walk to and fro

none are put off by my beauty.

The dark clouds in the distance dissipate   gather again

thunder is pressed down

searching persistently in the gaps between buildings

for emancipation.

The animals   are walking

the animals   are walking

the animals   are still walking.

Finally a great big animal

lying by my side, lets me touch

its ice-cold face

秘密花园

我和一群动物居住在一起

就我一个穿得干干净净。

它们走来走去

没人嫌弃我的美丽。

远处的乌云走了,又来了

雷声被压抑着

总想在楼宇的缝隙中

寻求解放。

动物,走着

动物,走着

动物,还走着。

最后一只大的动物

侧卧在我的身旁,让我用手

抚摸它冰凉的脸

It's Just That, at Center Stage, Slowly, Black Waters Gather

Death and Hope

what differentiates them

they're both dancers

both clad in tight black dresses

both surrounded by

the same dazzling reds

the same dazzling blues

the same dazzling yellows

Even their skeletons

like beautiful girls dazzlingly

open up. It's just that

at center stage, slowly, black waters gather.

只是，舞场中央慢慢积聚起黑色的水

死亡与希望

有什么区别

她们都是一个舞者

她们都穿着紧身的黑衣

她们的周围

有同样鲜艳的红

有同样鲜艳的蓝

有同样鲜艳的黄

即便是骷髅

也像美少女般鲜艳地

开放。只是

舞场中央慢慢积聚起黑色的水。

The Cartoon Deemed Ridiculous from the Start

As a matter of fact, I'm but a skeleton.

I'm not that horrifying.

I now climb into my own eyes,

where it's pitch-dark, but even if I jumped

I don't believe I'd fall

to my death.

卡通一开始就被定义为荒谬

实际上，我就是一具骷髅。

我没有那么狰狞。

我现在爬进我的眼睛，

里面一片漆黑，即便我从这里跳下

我也不相信我会

摔死。

Involvement with Sweet Death

Is like velvet

is like flowers woven with pubic hair

is like fairies

when they whisper

when they're completely unclothed and whisper.

与甜蜜死亡的干系

像丝绒一样

像阴毛编织的花朵

像仙女一样

当她们耳语

当她们脱光衣服耳语的时候。

We Are Playing Games Barefoot

Actually,

I'm not someone with a feel for language.

You cover my eyes,

you hold my hand, the right hand

moving left

on the left a candle is lit

on the left another candle is lit

on the left a third candle is lit.

I want to feel the light's heat,

to tell the first candle

from the second

from the third.

The person holding me has bright eyes,

she's embedded in the dark figure of shadow,

while I lean back against her breasts.

我们赤着脚在做游戏

实际上

我不是一个有语感的人。

你把我的眼蒙上,

你搀扶了我的手,右手

往左边去

左边有一支蜡烛已被点上

左边还有一支蜡烛已被点上

左边还有第三支蜡烛已被点上。

我要去寻找光的温度,

要分辨出第一支

第二支

和第三支。

搀扶我的人眼睛明亮,

她嵌在黑色的影像中,

而我,背依她的胸脯。

Waves Surprisingly Surge from Underneath

This is surely a real tree

it's burning in the sky

it delivers itself

to burn in the sky

it burns from its core

to its leaves and twigs

burns through the afternoon

burns through the black

in this burning

waves have surged from underneath

它的下面竟泛出波涛

这是一棵真树了

它在空中燃烧

它把自己

送到空中燃烧

从它的心烧起

到它的叶 它的枝桠

已经烧过了下午

已经烧过了黑色

在燃烧之中

它的下面已泛出波涛

You Put Yourself In

You're still like a human

but your wife seems like a fox

she comes forward to kiss you

she holds your chin between her paws

leans her body close

and sucks your tongue

her tail slowly pricks up

without turning a hair

soon it crosses her back

soon like the tongue of a flame

it quickly burns up to there

你把自己放了进去

你还像一个人

但你太太像一只狐狸

她走上前来吻你

她用前爪托起你的下巴

她附身凑近你

吸紧你的舌头

她把尾巴慢慢竖起

不动一点声色

很快越过她的后背

很快像一条火苗

迅速地烧到那里

Sincerity in the River's Morning Water

Boys, two boys

the boys sit by the river

the boys' palms protect their hearts

the boys, the moon shines on their backs

赤诚在早间的河水

男孩子,两个男孩子

男孩子,坐在河岸上

男孩子,手掌护着自己的心

男孩子,月亮照着他们的背

Hallucination

I've been waiting for her

the waterfall opened behind me

I've been waiting for her

the rose bloomed on my side

except for this wisp of whitish

diamond-shaped pink

no light

shines into

the phantom

that seized me

幻象

我等着她

身后的瀑布也开了

我等着她

身旁的玫瑰花也绽放了

除了这一缕白色和

菱形的粉红

什么光线

也没有照射进

攫取了我的

鬼魅

This Rock Would Like to Flower

Didn't expect you'd strip yourself naked, sitting so solemnly on a rock.

Didn't expect, sitting on a rock, you'd hold fresh flowers as such in your mouth.

You bare your body, sit upright

you are a goddess even if you're not a goddess.

This rock is heated by your lower body

this rock would like to flower.

这块石头想开花

不曾想你赤裸了身体如此庄严地坐在石头上。

不曾想你口衔如此鲜花坐在石头上。

你光了身体,端坐着

你不是女神也是女神了。

这块石头被你的下身所灼热

这块石头想开花。

Jump, Jump, Jump, Jump!

She's bound her legs to jump neatly into sex

she's tipped her toes to jump neatly into sex

she's raised her butt to the moonlight to jump neatly into sex

she dimmed her pink until shiningly pitch-black to jump neatly into sex

跳，跳，跳，跳！

她绑了自己的腿要整齐地跳进去

她踮了她的脚尖要整齐地跳进去

她抬起臀部让月光照耀要整齐地跳进去

她让粉色慢慢褪去直至黝黑发亮要整齐地跳进去

Kneeling or Crouching Sex

So-called cuteness was a woman's dream

she dreamt of her eyes turning blue

she dreamt of taking the sorrowful

pose of a peacock yet in the end she still dreamt of herself

becoming that simple animal capable of making love

跪着或趴下

所谓乖巧是一个女人的梦

她梦见自己的眼睛变蓝

她梦见自己摆了一个忧伤的

孔雀造型但最后她还是梦见了自己

变成的那个跪着或趴下的动物

A Poem Changes Direction While Writing

This muddy dirty face drops a piece each day

the eyes so beautiful the nose so beautiful as to grieve you

her lips open slightly inclined to speak this woman shrouded

in mud and dirt, still, I'd like to steal a kiss

一首诗在写作中改变了方向

污泥浊水的脸每天掉落一块

眼睛美得令人心疼鼻子美得也令人心疼

嘴唇微启着想要说话这女子尽管笼罩了

污泥浊水,我还是想偷偷地吻吻她

This Rotten Poem Is for Pound

I am indeed lonely

if death by loneliness is my punishment

three deaths are not enough

I miss light when there's no light

lift up my face as if to greet the thunder in the sky

actually it's for waiting for raindrops

the light drops down, section by section

when the eyes are used up use the muscles

when the chest is used up use the ankle

on the ground a pool of light gathers, like dust

it will fly away if blown

I adjust my steps carefully

and twirl my waist, lest the future

go broke tonight

oh Pound

把这首烂诗送给庞德

我的确孤独

孤独到死如果是惩罚

三个死也不够

没有光的时候想光

把脸颊迎上去仿佛迎向天上的雷声

实际上是为了等雨点

光一截截下来

用完了眼睛用肌肉

用完了胸脯用脚踝

地上积起的一摊光,如粉尘般

一吹就会飞走

我小心地合着我的脚步

旋着我的腰肢,不让未来

在今夜破产

庞德啊

Tense Relations

I didn't portray myself in any picture

my eyes were silent; in addition,

the train brushed past the picture. Startled I shield my chest

more surprised than anyone to find

in fact, I have no chest.

Your face is also made-up; I've no idea

whether it's expensive silver powder or cheap

junk, but when you smile

as if flowers bloom on the withered branch. Now I know how much

courage is needed

to write such a rotten poem

I didn't want to confront knowledge

I'm a cat— I lay in the bucket of pickled vegetables

or in the bin of left-over rice, showing others

      my bitter loneliness.

Finally, my face has a cat's splendor

all around my eyes covered with chalk marks,

stars and coins, each drop is shining

I won't burst into tears, I hold it in

I'm waiting for spring. When it comes,

don't mention the sky above my head, even

my belly, lower body and balls

will be studded with fresh flowers, as if the morning of heaven

suddenly opens its eyes.

紧张关系

我在每一幅画框中都不看我自己

我的眼睛是沉默的,加之

列车已经擦过画面。我吃惊地

掩护住我的胸脯时比谁都吃惊

事实上,我没有胸脯。

你的脸也是化过妆的,我不知道

是高贵的银粉还是廉价的

垃圾货,你笑的时候

仿佛是枯树枝上开放的

花瓣。现在我已知道

写一首烂诗需要何等勇气

我不想与知识形成对抗

我是猫呀,我躲在酸菜桶里

我躲在剩米箱里,让人

看到了我的孤苦无依。

我的脸上终于有了猫的灿烂

眼睛的周围被粉笔涂满

星星、钱币,一颗颗闪耀

我不流眼泪，我噙住

我要等到春天。到时候

不要说我的头顶、天空，就是

我的小腹、下身

也会缀满鲜花，像天堂的早晨

突然睁开了眼睛。

Love in Despair

I was in the shape of a ring, a snake

I was not able to walk out. The crowd surrounding me

held flowers and cheese in their hands

as if they were comforting a patient

so many people looked like gentlemen

people in black top hats

people in black scarves

why so many.

I was in the dark and still saw you

you bared your upper body, twirling crazily

you already bumped against the edge of the wall.

Caught, you caught the wall,

caught, you caught a hooting light,

the fence is growing around me

in the speed of spring, although she has

no idea what she's growing. Still,

I'm in the shape of a ring, a snake

but now even smaller, more bewitching, herrr…

the pity and loneliness of all pictures

are concentrated here

a late portrait of love is worshiped

on the table full of rotten flowers; only one person

in dark sunglasses is looking at me

and chanting, half-heartedly, despair

绝望爱情

我处于环形之中，是蛇

我已走不出去。围观我的人群

手持了鲜花、奶酪

仿佛慰藉一个病号。

那么多绅士一样的人，

戴着黑色礼帽的人，

围着黑色围巾的人，

怎么那么多。

我在黑暗中，还是看见了你

你赤裸着上体，疯狂旋转着

已经撞上墙沿。

抓住，你抓住墙壁了

抓住，你抓住鸣叫的灯了，

而栅栏在我四围成长

春天的速度，尽管她

并不知道成长什么。我

仍处于环形之中，是蛇

却已变得更小、更妖，嘀

在所有画面中的孤独与可怜

都已集中到了这里

爱情的遗像被供奉在

烂花铺满的桌面，只有一人

戴着墨镜，看着我

假惺惺地吟诵着绝望。

Offer Modigliani a Subject

A woman

came up with a method to handle a panther. She

puts on a tiger head

dons tiger clothes

she's now a tiger

she can communicate with the panther

be with the panther as an equal

the panther likes her apparel, likes

the zippers inlaid all over her body

the panther knows, this tiger has got it all,

alcohol, marijuana,

and sex too

"Step by step, the humans

migrate into animals, is this ultimately

a good thing or not?"

The panther decides

without being clear on this point,

there'll be no blood bath.

送莫迪里阿尼一个题材

有一个女人

想了个办法对付豹子,她

戴上了虎头

穿上了虎的衣衫

她就是一头虎了

她可以与豹子交流

平等地与豹子在一起

豹子喜欢她的装束喜欢

她镶满全身的拉链

豹子知道,这只老虎什么都有

有酒精,有大麻

还有性

"人类一步一步地

迁徙到动物中来,这究竟

是好事还是坏事?"

豹子决计

在没有想明白这一点之前

它不血淋淋。

The Height of the Master Almost Reaches the Eaves

A craftsman carves some pieces of wood into a Master

they're painted black to show the existence of a soul

they're painted with grease paint to show the heart's purity

they doesn't pee, only sweats in summer

大师的身高已快接近房檐

有一些木头被匠人刻成了大师

它们被涂上黑色即表示有了灵魂

它们被刷上油彩则表示内心淳美

它们不小便　只在夏天沁出些汗

The Mortality of Happiness Is Twice That of Loneliness

Can loneliness cause death? Someone tells me. Yes.
For three days I bang bang on the wall and I'm not lonely
I make the toilet gurgle gurgle and I'm not lonely. The fourth day
in the floor appears a hole "Happiness causes death"

快乐死亡率高于孤独一倍

孤独会导致死亡吗　有人告诉我，会。
三天来我把墙壁敲得咚咚响我不孤独
我把马桶搞得哗哗响我不孤独　第四天
地板上出现了一个洞"快乐导致死亡"

Counteraction

My wishes part from me.

They brush past my shoulder,

walking to my back.

My back shines a dim light, which is melancholic, gloomy,

and obscure, but extremely beautiful.

I hold my breath. My eyes express the effort to move forward,

but bewildered stand heavily in place, motionless.

反制

我的愿望正离我而去。

她们与我擦肩而过,

走向我的背面。

我的背面透射着昏黄的灯光,忧郁,昏暗,

晦涩,但它美极了。

我屏住呼吸。我的眼神试图向前,

但迷惘总是沉甸甸地立于原地。一动不动。

All Protection Lost

I'm watching the black smoke in the distance

this darkness already bigger than the houses

this darkness already bigger than the trees

this darkness already bigger than half the sky

this darkness already bigger than

my nearby flustered body

unable to move one step forward

所有的庇护都在丧失

我望着远处的黑烟

它的黑暗已大过了房屋

它的黑暗已大过了树

它的黑暗已大过了半个天空

它的黑暗已大过了

近处的我的慌张的身体

无法往前挪动一步

Misappropriation, My Scheme

My viciousness hasn't left me.

Two black cloth strips

cover my eyes.

I'm not someone arrogantly closing myself off

I'm struggling

leaving the whites of my eyes outside.

Struggling, not just my heart, hands and feet,

but even the whites of my eyes.

The whites of my eyes open,

    as if the body were blooming,

as if my whole body were full with open wings.

挪用，我的预谋

我的狠毒没有离开我。

两根黑色的布条

遮蔽了我的眼睛。

我不是封闭到自高自大的人

我挣扎着

把眼白留在外面。

挣扎着，不只意味着内心、手脚，

它已经到了眼白。

我的眼白开放着，

像开放的身体，

像全身开满了翅膀。

Tattoo

I'm holding this hand in my mouth.

Because of the effort, my cheeks crack a bit.

This hand   is very gorgeous,

I can't say it's unclean.

But it's possibly killed someone.

The fingernails are deathly pale, as if

soaked in formaldehyde.

I'm holding this hand.

Because of the effort, my cheeks crack,

the core of the crack is the part that breaths hard.

刺青

我衔着这只手。

由于用力,我的脸颊有些开裂了。

这只手,它很艳丽,

我不能说它不干净。

它可能杀过人。

它的指甲惨白得仿佛

浸泡在福尔马林。

我衔着这只手。

由于用力,我的脸颊有些开裂了,

开裂的核心,是用力吸气的部分。

Connection

Jump into a clock for a swim.

Jump into a sea for a holiday.

Such a trip in time

as if the blue were fed up by a dog.

联系

跳进一只钟里游泳。

跳进一只海里度假。

这样的时光之旅,

像蓝色被狗喂得饱饱的。

Predicament

A man

grasped an eagle in his hand,

they

stared long at each other

An eagle

grasped a woman in its hand,

they

also stared long at each other.

困境

一男人

将一只鹰握在手里，

他和它

对视了很久。

一只鹰

将一女人握在手里，

它和她

也对视了很久。

Blood-colored Jam

I'll first affirm

that this is a fairy,

but she doesn't want to be a fairy.

This jam

already smeared over

her lips, neck and chest,

as a drop trickles on her breast

she quietly makes the sign of the cross

血色之果酱

我先肯定

这是一仙女儿,

但她不要做仙女。

这些果酱

已经吐满

她的嘴唇、脖颈和胸口,

当有一枚滴沥到她的乳房时

她轻轻地画了个十字

Love in the Last Glow of Sunset

Oh my!

I'm the one standing in seawater playing a guitar.

A refined woman walks by.

Two refined women walk by.

Three refined women walk by.

Nobody listens to my music.

Nobody throws me a penny.

Oh my!

爱在落日余晖

乖乖。

我是站在海水里弹吉他的那个人。

一个斯文的女人走过我的面前。

两个斯文的女人走过我的面前。

三个斯文的女人走过了我的面前。

没有人聆听我的音乐。

没有人投掷硬币。

乖乖。

Enter You, Just As Anxiety Finds a Wonderful Dream

My dog and I are friends

my dog and I are brothers

my dog and I work together

my dog and I farm together

my dog and I fly in the sky

my dog and I dive in the water

we curse each other: "I'll rip your ass!"

whereas, when it comes time to die

we can't say goodbye

进入你，就像焦虑找到了美梦

我和我的狗是朋友

我和我的狗是兄弟

我和我的狗一起做工

我和我的狗一起耕地

我和我的狗在空中飞翔

我和我的狗在水中潜水

我们互相诅咒："我要撕裂你的屁股！"

然而是死亡的时候了

我们却无法说再见

To Sarah Kane

Blood flowed through the instep

Blood flowed through the instep

Blood flowed through the instep

Due to normal biological imperative

people are satisfied with listening to

moans in the toilet

致萨拉·凯恩

血 流过了脚背

血 流过了脚背

血 流过了脚背

人们只因正常的生理

而满足于倾听

马桶里的呻吟

Reaction

I show my breast in 10 pages

I show my breast for 10 days

I show my breast in 10 pages for 10 days

I have met you 100 times,

Do you still think there's only one breast?

反应

我在 10 页纸上展示了我的乳房。

我有 10 天展示了我的乳房。

我有 10 天在 10 页纸上展示了我的乳房。

我在 10 页纸上我有 10 天展示了我的乳房。

我与你见面 100 次了,

你仍然只觉着是 1 只乳房吗?

To Godard

Birds   are flying in the flood

in the waves

birds   are bunched together

beaks pressed to beaks

wings pressed to wings

film like a fence,

can't block

the red sea

white can smother you

green extends death

Godard

You're a gold bead

tightly held in the birds' beaks

致戈达尔

鸟 飞翔在洪水

在浪潮

鸟 相互簇拥

鸟喙压迫鸟喙

翅膀压迫翅膀

胶片如栅栏

不能拦住

红海洋

白色尽可让你窒息

绿色延展死亡

戈达尔

你是鸟喙衔紧的

一枚金珠

Border: To Bei Dao

Stealthily

what chance does it seek

what chance does desire seek

what chance does greed seek

what chance does loyalty seek

what chance does heroism seek

the white of day extends

behind you

边界：致北岛

悄悄地

它在伺机什么

欲望在伺机什么

贪婪在伺机什么

忠诚在伺机什么

英勇在伺机什么

白天 已经扩大到

你的身后

Bright Reality

They're kids

sleeping in the wheat field

indeed, they're just

wheat seeds

clutched in your hands

明亮的现实

他们是

睡在 麦地里的孩子

他们原本就是

握在你们手里的

麦粒

Vivacious Body

In the sky above the wheat field

birds   fly

People in the wheat field

form lines

They blame themselves

Why are their palms so thick

Why are their buttocks so sturdy

Why are their legs so heavy

Only a child riding on shoulders

Still thinks of flying

昂扬的身体

麦地上空的

鸟啊 飞吧

麦地里的

人啊 排成长队

他们自责

为什么手掌如此粗大

为什么臀部如此坚实

为什么双腿如此沉重

只有一个骑在肩上的小孩

还想飞

Eavesdropping on the Soul

There are two strips of

black shadow

one stays on the wall

the other stays on the back

偷听灵魂

有两条

黑色的影子

一条留在墙壁上

一条留在后背上

Fragile

Who can protect you

even the flight

of folded paper

frightens you

out of your wits

脆弱

谁能保护你

连一只

折纸的飞行

都使你

惊恐万状

Irrigation Is the Lifeblood of Agriculture

A big tree caught fire

we poured water on the roots

a great mountain caught fire

we led water to the valley

the ground caught fire

we filled the underground with water

what have we done wrong

just that we're stupid

water managers

If The Wheat Dies

100

水利是农业的命脉

大树着火

我们往树根浇水

大山着火

我们往山谷引水

大地着火

我们往地下灌水

我们做错了什么

只因我们是愚蠢的

水利员

Lowly

The lizard remains on the chair back

one day

two days

three days

the lizard still remains on the chair back

卑微

蜥蜴留在椅背上

一天

二天

三天

蜥蜴仍然留在椅背上

Grace

Crack the wound open

there's singing inside

crack the wound open

there's dancing inside

crack the wound open

there're crowds of people

rushing in and out

one after another, they're licking

the wound painted over with candy

恩泽

掰开伤口

里面有歌唱

掰开伤口

里面有舞蹈

掰开伤口

里面有成群结队的人

涌进又涌出

他们轮番舔舐着

用糖果画成的伤口

Snow Piled Up on the Mountains

A flock of birds

in the mountains

and a fly

in a pile of paper

What's the difference?

Nothing.

白雪已积满群山

在群山

中的鸟群,

与纸堆

中的苍蝇,

有何不同?

没有。

Part-timer Chicks Come Here in Spring

Two chicks in winter

look like politicians

on the down of their breasts

are painted two napkins

but no one serves them

打工的小鸟春天来

冬天里的两只鸟

像政客

它们胸前的绒毛

被油漆成 两块餐布

却无人伺候

Red Memory

Red

is a memory

though rusty, the golden color

upholds its majesty

the child not once attempted to cover the scarlet

he always jumps in and out

through the small side door

红的记忆

红

是一种记忆

金色即便锈蚀

也坚持着威严

孩子 从未企图抹煞鲜红

总是从旁边的小门

跳进跳出

A Crane Rests on the Roof

Each of us   has

a dwelling in the sky

incessantly we

climb up

the wind

has rip our shirts

and then tears our pants

仙鹤歇在房顶

我们 都有

一处房子在空中

我们不停地

攀爬

风沙先是

撕破了我们的上衣

又撕扯我们的裤子

To Kerouac

A palette

tipped over

on a clock face

what time stirs

most

is still the black

致凯鲁亚克

调色盘

打翻在钟面上

时间掀起

最多的

还是黑色

Zidane

Melancholic in the rose of flame

Zidane and Zidane   separate

playing their own balls

four Zidanes are running

three Zidanes are running

two Zidanes are running

separately, only one Zidane

the Zidane in the heart

is melancholic in the rose of flame

so lonely that he can only see

the Zidane of the heart

the ball   has become a nuisance

齐内

忧郁在焰火的玫瑰

齐内与齐内 各自分开

踢各自的球

四个齐内在奔走

三个齐内在奔走

二个齐内在奔走

各自分开，只有一个

在内心中的齐内

忧郁在焰火的玫瑰

孤独到了只看见

内心的齐内

球，已变成了一个累赘

Yoko Ono[*]

If you watch her close up

She's a mountain

She's an ocean

if you blow a puff of air

she'll dance in the wind

小野洋子

你靠近了她看

她就是山

就是海洋

你轻轻吹一口气

她就迎风招展

---

[*] The Chinese characters of the name Yoko Ono literally mean "Small wilderness, Tiny Ocean."

The Flame's Distortion

a conflagration   it

can't burn to the outside

can't even penetrate glass

it lets the thick smoke smother the big fire

lets the big fire

struggle once or twice

like a penis

火焰的篡改

一场大火　它

烧不到外面去

甚至穿不过玻璃

它让浓烟窒息大火

它让大火

像阴茎一样　还有

一二次的挣扎

A Narrow Staircase

I arrive by escalator on the fourth floor

a security camera

pointed right at me from above

It's so close

that I stick the chewing-gum in my mouth

on its lens

Old Gao, who follows right behind, asks

"why did you stick your chewing-gum

on the lens?"

I answer with titter, "Because it's too close."

一架窄梯

我上扶梯到四楼时

一只摄像头

顶头对准了我

因为很近

我就把嘴里的口香糖

贴在了它的镜头上

跟上来的老高问

"你为什么要把口香糖

贴在它的镜头上"

我答"呵呵,因为很近啊"

Neither Bright Nor Upright

Surely lured by a demon or a spirit

I did something like this:

I got to the Square, got to

one side of the Square, got to

the center of the side of the Square

I picked out one of the "Flowery Lanterns" *

earnestly counted its security cameras

"Wow, so many!"

there were at least thirteen.

I'm scared the person behind the camera might see me

so I raised my fingers pretending

to be counting the gardenias on the Flowery Lantern.

---

* the "flowery lanterns" are the multi-headed light posts which illuminate large urban spaces in Chinese cities.

不光明正大

一定是鬼使神差

我才做了这样的事情：

我到了广场，到了

广场边，到了

广场边的中央

我选择了一株"华灯"

认真地数了数它上面的

摄像头，"噢，真多呀，"

起码有十三个。

我怕摄像头里的人看到我

我举起手指，假装

我在数着华灯上的白兰花。

This Is the Biggest Horse I Saw Today

She is one head higher than the others in the long, long line

she wears   golden hair   formal suit   short skirt   white blouse

standing in a Shanghai line, her legs

seem like two cylinders   two sticks of metal   two pieces of

music

you sense that she's invincible

the time when people are enclosed by rain, snow, and haze

is longer than this line

her presence stirs people's hearts

the Shanghai people have an outlet now

one realizes that uttering the soft tones of the Shanghai dialect

is a shame

the big tall horse

is actually just the one with golden hair   formal suit   white

blouse   short skirt

her two legs

draw your eyes upward

you'll hear phonographs singing   and the spring

这是今天看到的最大的马

她在长长的队伍中高出队伍一头

她 金发 正装 短裙 白衬衫

她的两腿站立在上海的队伍中

仿佛两根圆柱 两只金属 两支乐曲

你感受她是不可战胜的

人们被雨雪 阴霾封闭的时间

已经比这支队伍要长得多

她的出现搅乱了人心

上海人也有住口的时候了

有人意识到发出吴侬软语是一种耻辱

高大的马儿

实际上就是一头金发 正装 白衬衫 短裙

她的两腿

如果牵引你的视线往上走

你会听到留声机 轰鸣 和春天

Airport Railway Express

Go deeper

Pound disappears

and deeper

Pound disappears

and deeper

Pound disappears

and deeper

Pound disappears

what branch

or flower

机场快轨

往深处去

庞德不见了

往深处去

庞德不见了

往深处去

庞德不见了

往深处去

庞德不见了

什么枝桠

与花朵

I Need Something Dry

Semi-circular face

is inside the copper coin

woods

is inside the face

fruit

is inside the woods

face

is inside

the fruit

我需要一些干燥的东西

半圆的面孔

在铜板之中

树林在

面孔之中

果实在

树林之中

面孔又在

果实

之中

The Green Monster

Playing accordion, the old man stands by the door

his two legs stand by the door

his hands stand by the door

his nearsighted glasses stand by the door

the accordion stands by the door

the green on the accordion stands by the door

the snow on the accordion stands by the door

as the green monster

leading a group of old men

jumps happily outside the door

绿怪兽

拉手风琴的老人站在门边

他的双腿站在门边

他的手站在门边

他的近视眼镜站在门边

手风琴站在门边

手风琴上的绿站在门边

手风琴上的雪站在门边

而绿怪兽

带着一大帮老人在门外

开心地跳

Going Up to Yunnan

Mushrooms also bloom

black patterns bloom

white patterns bloom

crosses bloom

ridges bloom

terraces bloom

clouds also bloom

上云南

蘑菇也开放

黑色的纹理在开放

白色的纹理在开放

十字在开放

山脊在开放

梯田在开放

云也开放

Jaipur

A pitiful heart

wrapped up in a tiny body

a tiny body

wrapped up in red hair

red hair

wrapped up in horrified eyes

eyes

She only stares at   death

斋浦尔

可怜的心

被包裹在小小的身体里

小小的身体

被包裹在红发里

红色头发

被包裹在惊恐的眼睛里

眼睛

她只死盯住 死

Paris

I want

this kind of woman

her diamonds can fly

her alluring beak   goes down

Paris lights her up

with the golden color of dusk

巴黎

我要

这样的女人

珠宝也会飞翔

诱人的长喙 向下

巴黎用黄昏的金色

把她照亮

Goddess

She can regard me as a mask

she can regard me as a corpse

but when I look at her, she is so fresh

as if her breasts were spring water

about to slide out of the picture.

神

她可以把我看成是一副面具

她可以把我看成是一具尸体

而我看她时，她鲜活得

胸乳也仿佛春水

就快从画面的中心滑落出来。

I've slept with the Sea

I've Slept with the Sea.

With my body, my sturdiness

and my sex.

"I've slept with the Sea!"

This is

the nonsense

I utter under the heat of the sun in the tone of a northerner

who as if has just conquered the sea.

There's a woman, fat but robust and pretty,

wrapped in colorful satin

like a peacock; she passed by

offering a challenge.

I'm practically naked, spread out over the sandy beach.

Then, she also becomes almost naked, spreads out over

the sandy beach.

This woman's extremely vulgar beauty

I take, amazingly enough, as the sun's beauty

the blue sky's beauty and the sea's beauty.

"I've slept with the sea!"

When the dense sand covers my back

my legs, my bottom, my hands, my neck

and my breath, I don't feel lyrical at all

the pressure concentrated in my lower body

as if another wave roars

loudly making love.

我睡过大海

我睡过大海。
用我的身体,我的坚实
和我的性。
"我睡过大海!"
这是
我在炙热的阳光下以一个
封闭的北方人的口吻发出
的貌似已经征服了大海的
胡话。
有一个肥胖但结实也漂亮
的女人紧裹孔雀一样斑斓
的纱丽,她走过我的身旁
已形成挑衅。
我几乎全裸,覆盖在沙滩上。
接着,她也几乎全裸,覆盖在沙滩上。
这女人极其庸俗的美,
竟让我看成这就是太阳的美
蓝天的美,大海的美。

"我睡过大海!"

当密集的沙粒覆盖我的背部

我的腿我的臀我的手我的颈

我的呼吸的时候,

我没有感到一丝抒情

沉重聚集在我的下身

仿佛又一阵海浪呼啸

嘿咻嘹亮。

Decorating Ourselves as Tanks, We Wouldn't Look for Love

We're fully decorated

creeping on the ground

on the ground are several hedgehogs

red hedgehogs

black hedgehogs

hedgehogs of different colors

I dress her and myself up

as two hedgehogs

we're listening to something

we're waiting for a chance to do something bad

her skirt   is already too dirty

to look at

as for her sex

she no longer cares about that

把自己包装成坦克一样，就不打算恋爱了

我们穿着盛装

匍匐在地上

地上 有一些刺猬

红色的刺猬

黑色的刺猬

不同颜色的刺猬

我把自己和她

也打扮成两只刺猬

我们聆听着什么

我们伺机干点坏事

她的裙子 脏得

已经不堪入目

性别对她来说也

已不在乎

Meaning and Horse

One can always find something that seems a horse

" 象 ", a Chinese character.* Its big elephant trunk

starts to lead me. I find my mane

my head, my throat, my ears and

   my body

which also seems a light eaten away

or a sliding cut short

or a piece of wood firmly bitten

when it turns its head and takes off

I plop to my death on a ground of moon light

Death. This is no longer merely something that seems

a horse.

---

*   The meanings of the word 象 are: 1) to seem; 2) image; 3) elephant

语义和马

总能找到一些像马的事物

"像",一个汉字。巨大的鼻子

它开始牵引我。找到了我的鬃

我的头,我的喉,我的耳和

   我的身

就又像被噬去的光亮

就又像被砍断的滑行

就又像被紧紧咬住的一块木头

它掉头而去

我在一片月亮地上,伏地倒毙

死。这就不仅仅是一些像马的

事物

Grammar

Beginning from the rear of the car

start to disassemble the car's parts one by one

at which step of the disassembly

can the car no longer run away

语法

从汽车的尾部

挨次拆下汽车的零件

拆到第几步

汽车不能开走

Silent Fantasy

A drop of water

fell from up on the scaffold

I don't know how it can

climb back up

平静的异想

一滴水

从脚手架上跌下来

我不知道，它

怎样才能爬上去

Different from Trains that I Saw

The train goes deep into my dream

the whistle sings woooh woooh

what stays are the wheels

what drives away are the cars

和我见到的列车不一样

火车深入我的梦境

汽笛呜呜响

留下的是轮子

开走的是车厢

Untitled

A friend invites me out to the eastern suburbs

"Hey, bring your bride with you!"

then, I saw

a bird with a red mole

crawling on a leaf

无题

朋友约我到东郊郊游

"喂,带上新娘!"

接着,我就看到了

一只长有红痣的

鸟,匍匐在叶上

Copulating Ants

Copulating ants

some green some red. Like race car riders

they overturn the happy land

to the ground

交媾的蚂蚁

交媾的蚂蚁

红红绿绿。像赛车的骑手

把快乐的土地

掀翻在地

Joyful Things

After getting up in the morning

I pull open the curtain

this is a joyful thing

I do just like everyone else

the sunshine pours into my room

the sunshine falls on my wife's face

at this moment

my wife

simple lines

light body

I can't imagine

any deep place in her as a woman

a bird

drops to the windowsill

a gust of wind

lifts the bird's wings

a wintry autumn leaf

gently, rolls the wind

欢乐的事情

早晨起来

我把窗帘拉开

这是我做的和大家一样

欢乐的事情

阳光涌进我的房间

阳光落在我妻子的脸上

这一时刻

我的妻子

线条简洁

身体轻盈

我再也想象不出

作为女人她深刻的地方

有一只鸟儿

落在窗台上

有一阵风

掀动起鸟儿的翅膀

有一片秋冬的叶子

又把风轻轻卷起

Feeding

Carrying a wooden bucket

Shouldering a copper ladle

I feed the pigeons,

yet I know

to feed the pigeons

doesn't require

a wooden bucket

or a copper ladle

but take a look at

those grand people

on the grand street

and their exaggerated looks

    the same as mine

喂食

提着一只木桶

掮着一根铜勺

我给鸽子喂食的时候

就已知道

给鸽子喂食

并不需要

提着一只木桶

掮着一根铜勺

但是你看看

大路上

那些高高大大的人们

和我一样夸张的神色

The Play at the Kaiming Theatre

A fake man dresses himself up as a real man

a real man can't tell he's a fake

they go hand in hand, in step

one person plucks flowers with the left hand

the other plucks flowers with the right

nobody can tell true from false

they go hand in hand, in step

until they encounter a river

the fake man doesn't know he should wear boots

the real man doesn't know he can ford the river barefoot

the two men shake their heads on opposite sides, going

their separate ways

开明剧场的戏剧

一个假人把自己打扮得像真人一样

一个真人已认不出他是假人

他们手挽手,步调一致

一个人用左手采花

一个人用右手采花

没有人能辨出真假

他们手挽手,步调一致

直到经过一条河

假人不知道应该穿上靴子

真人不知道光着脚也能过河

两人在两岸摇摇头,分了手

Passing Rain-Flower Terrace

With hair dripping wet

look for those people holding torches high

ride up onto the wall of the Terrace mound

"Hey—" ask a question of these

people digging upstones

经过雨花台

头发上滴着水

找一找那些高举火把的人

骑上岗上的那道墙

"喂——"问一问这些

挖着石头的人

Imitate Classical Philosophy

On the altar

the porcelain vase and

the bird exchange wings ceaselessly

such will pierce your

      stagnant eyes

仿古典哲理

祭坛上

这样的：瓷花瓶和

鸟不停地交换着翅膀

会刺伤你们

停滞的眼睛

Fake Aphorism

The road paved with gold

has no room for your feet

伪格言

金子铺路的地方

踏不下自己的脚

Greedy Sheep

I give you my mouth

my tongue is hard bitten

the world becomes so splendid

a shaft of red light

encircles the meadow

the one riding the gold-engraved armchair

certainly is a greedy sheep

贪婪的羊

把我的嘴唇给你

咬紧我的舌头

天地间变得如此辉煌

一片红光

包围着草地

骑在那把镂金交椅上的

肯定是一只贪婪的羊

Our Country's Agriculture

About agriculture, I say

Grain

Maize

Yams

Pomegranates

Budding cardamom

Wheat

Wheat (Wheat is law)

Rats that walk in stacks of wheat

Raise a slogan: 'Defend wheat'

(Note: No work, no food)

Agriculture breeds sharp teeth.

From a distance people look at cows and sheep in groups, wheat blooming,

this is a tender heart indeed.

我国农业

关于农业,我说

1. 粮食

2. 玉米

3. 红薯

4. 石榴

5. 豆蔻初绽

6. 小麦

7. 小麦(小麦就是法律)

8. 小麦堆里穿行的老鼠

9. 提出口号:"保卫小麦"

(附注:不劳动者不得食)

农业哺育了尖利的牙齿。

人们遥望牛羊成群,小麦开花

这却是温柔的心灵

Ride a Jet

The down flying in the sky

the green down

I dreamt of you

In this endless sky

you, the flying down

are kids skipping school

green down

I want to stretch my foot out of the jet

my shoe looks like a red fruit

it brings to you our amazing world

my mother, brothers, and sisters

my father, as well

they all stand in a line

in a golden wheat field

watching us flying

like the planes in our sky

you, the flying down

I love you all and you

should also stick tight

to me, to my brother singing

down, down, down

乘坐喷气式飞机

天空中飞翔的绒毛

绿色的绒毛

我梦见你们

这是经历不完的天空

你们,飞翔的绒毛

逃学的孩子

绿色的绒毛

我要把脚伸出机舱外

我的鞋子像一只红色的水果

它带给你们我们神奇的世界

我的母亲、弟弟、妹妹、姐姐

还有父亲

他们站成一队

在一片金黄的麦地上

像我们天空中的飞机

注视着我们的飞行

你们,飞翔的绒毛

我爱着你们你们

也要顽强地贴紧着我

贴紧着我的兄弟的歌唱

绒毛，绒毛，绒毛

Fresh Wood

A row of logs flies in the sky

plummets down, what break apart

first is the wind

next, is still the wind

新鲜的木材

一排木材从天上飞过

砸下来,砸断的

首先是风

其次,还是风

Behavioral Error

If someone paint us

completely blood red

then throw us on the snowy ground.

The snowy ground has a slope

but we're not covered over by snow.

Then let's just listen:

"Wow, a beautiful wreath!"

"Wow, what a circle!"

"Wow, giant fragments of humankind!"

Fragments, an extreme judgment

and yet we're simply disguised as

fruit in winter. Nobody think this way.

行为的过失

假如,把我们这些人

涂满了血红的颜色。

把我们扔置在雪地。

雪地有一块斜坡

而我们并不被雪覆盖

我们就听着吧:

"呵,一个美丽的花环!"

"呵,这样的圆圈!"

"呵,人类巨大的碎片!"

碎片,一个极而言之的评价

而我们只是伪装成

冬天的果子。没有人这样认为

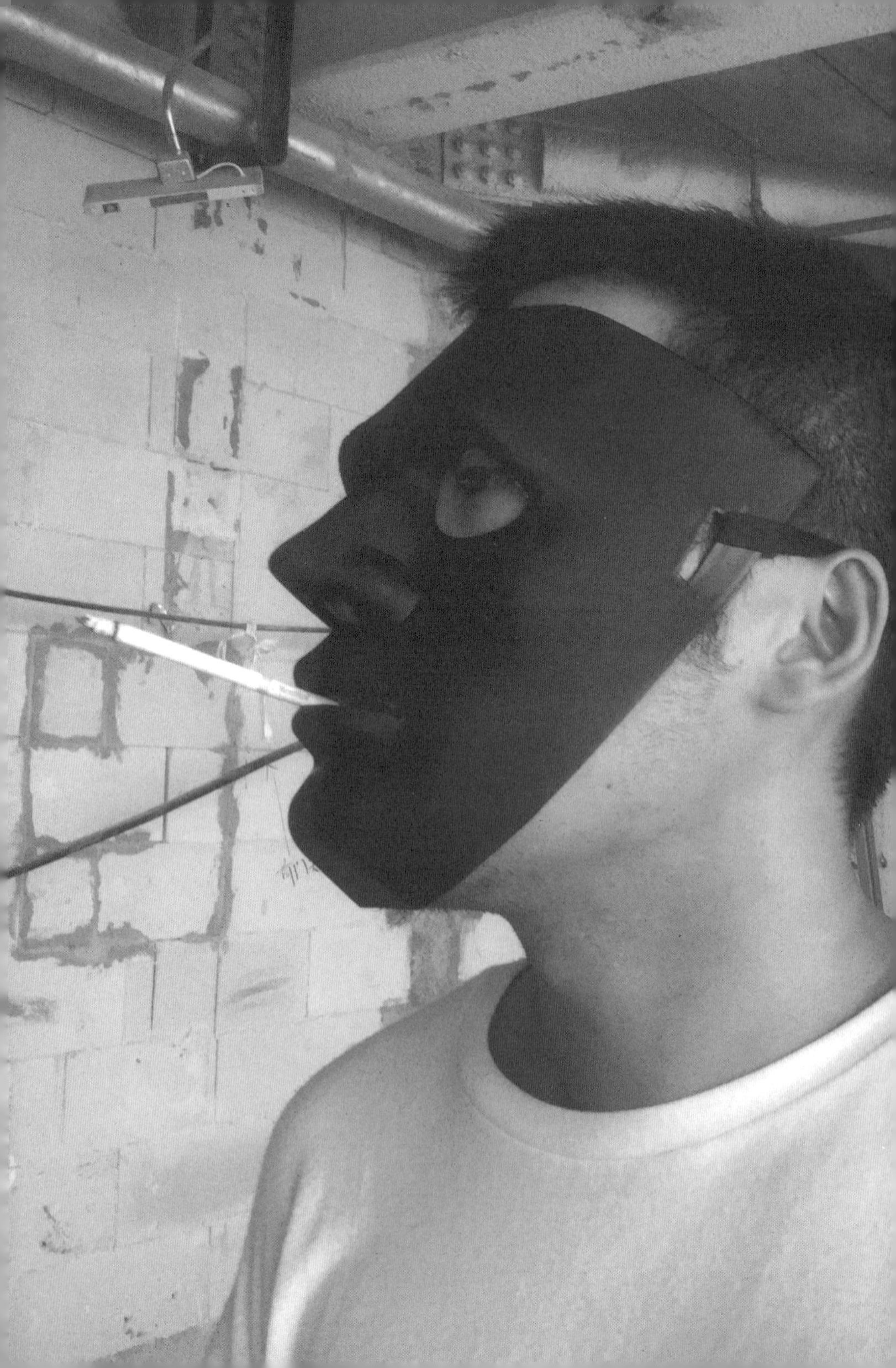

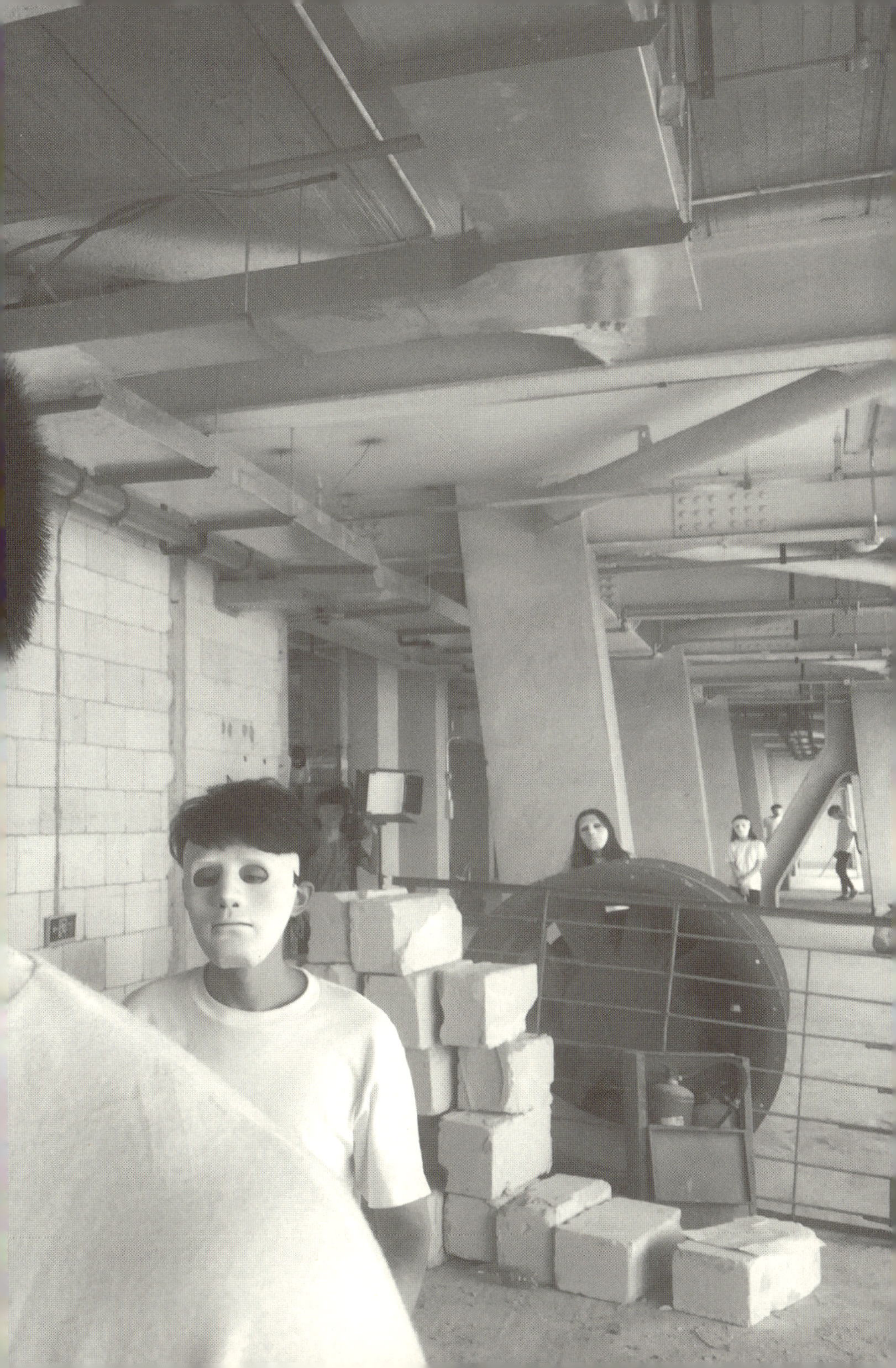

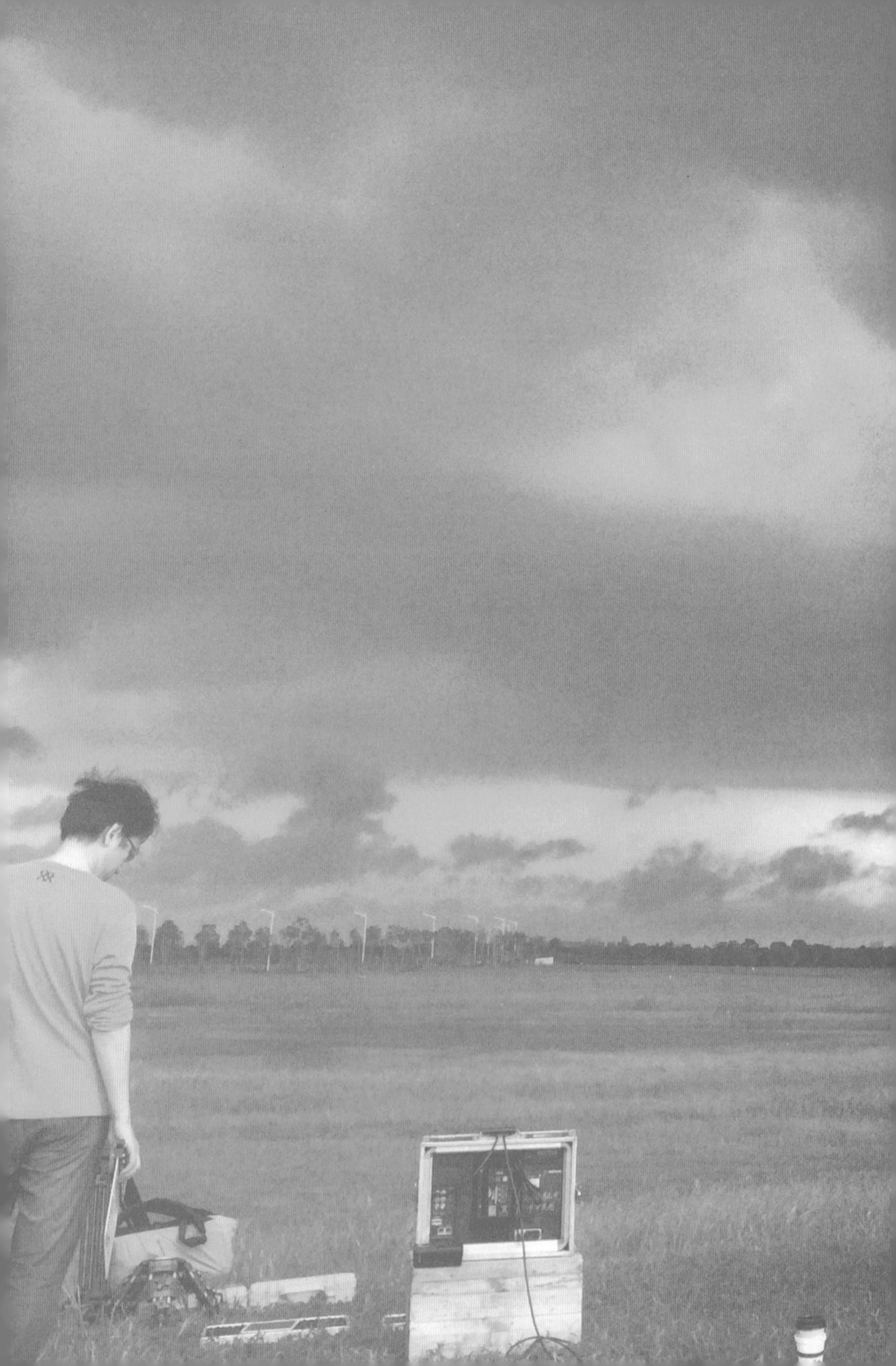

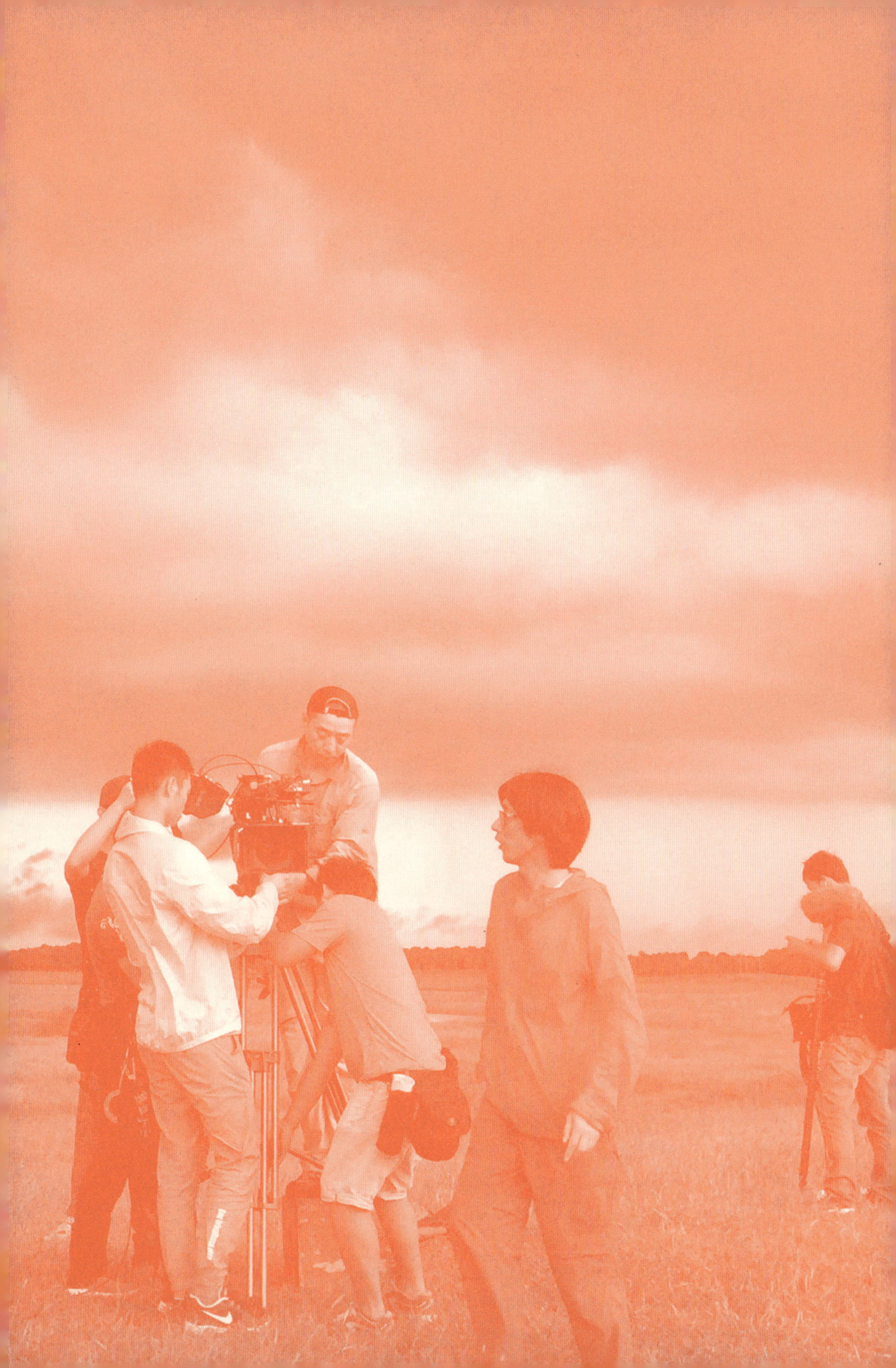

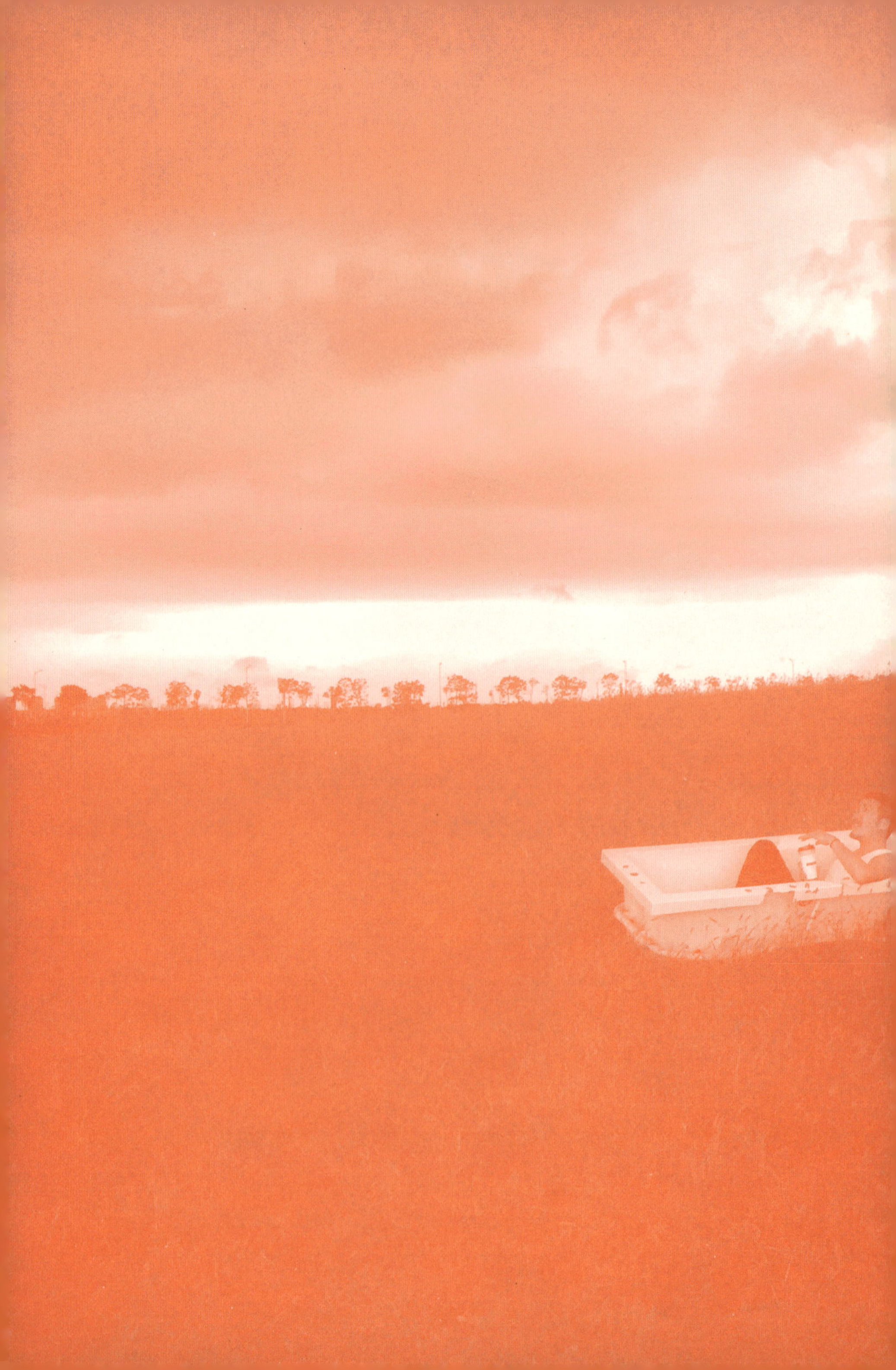

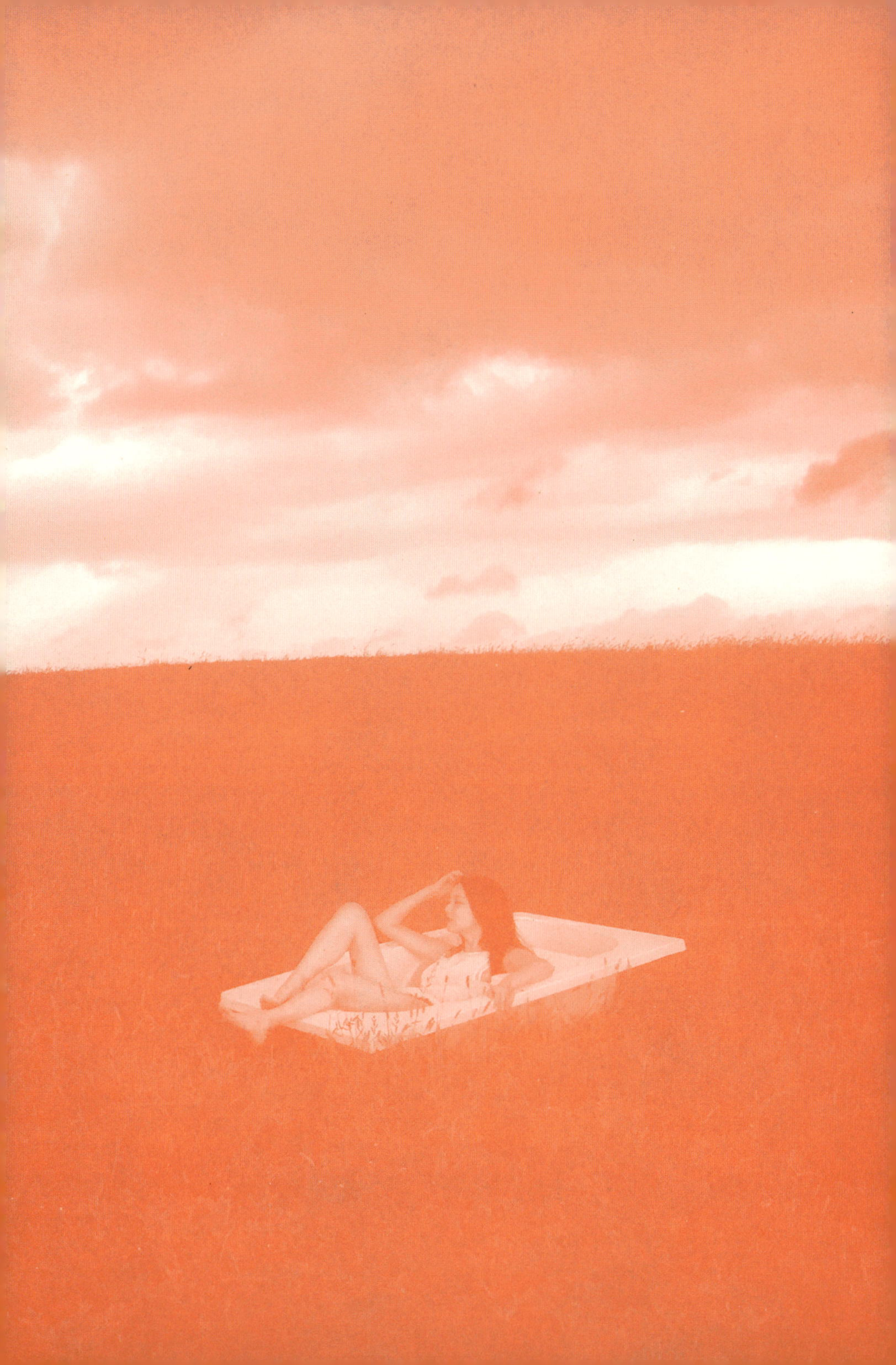

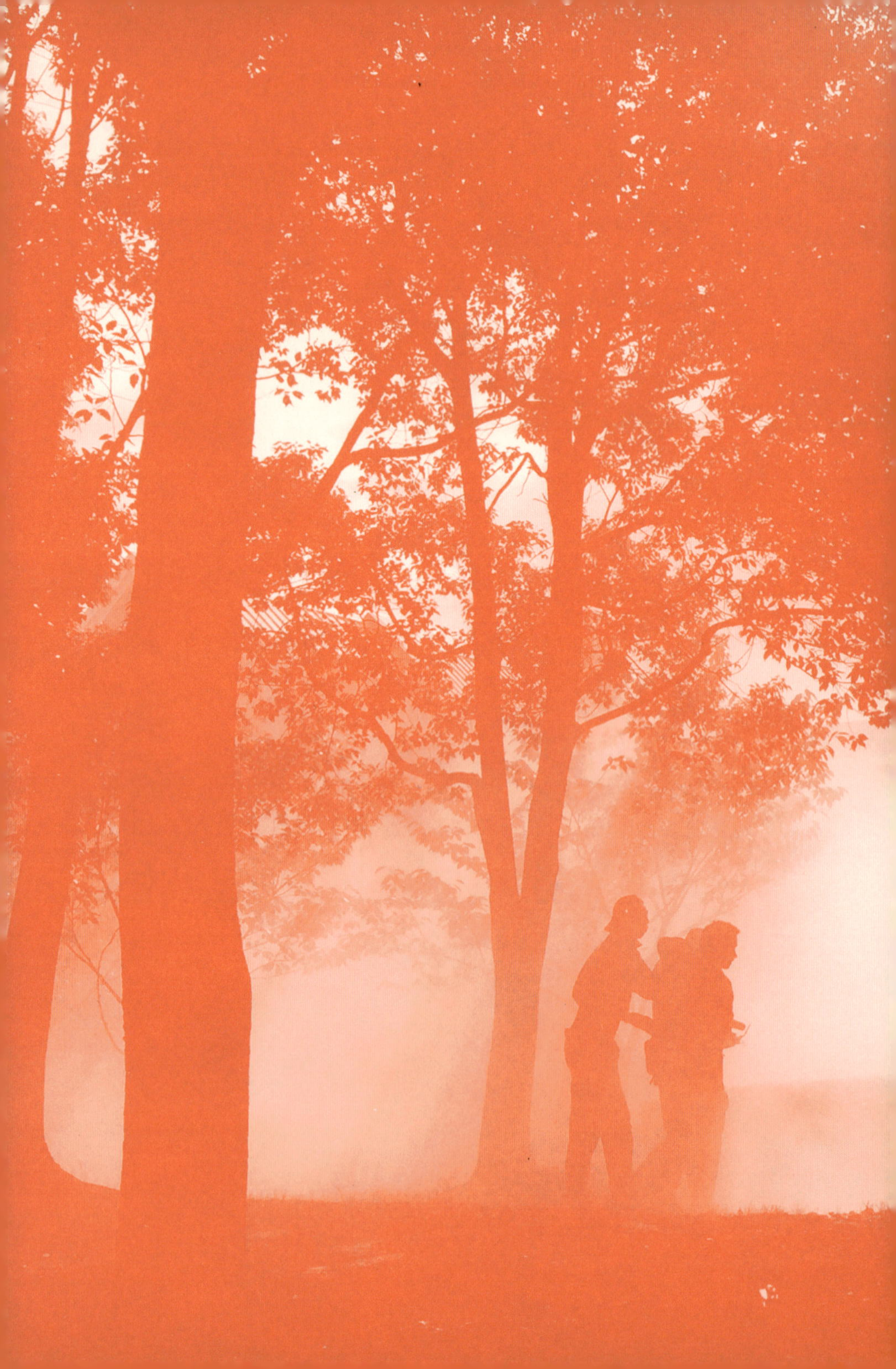

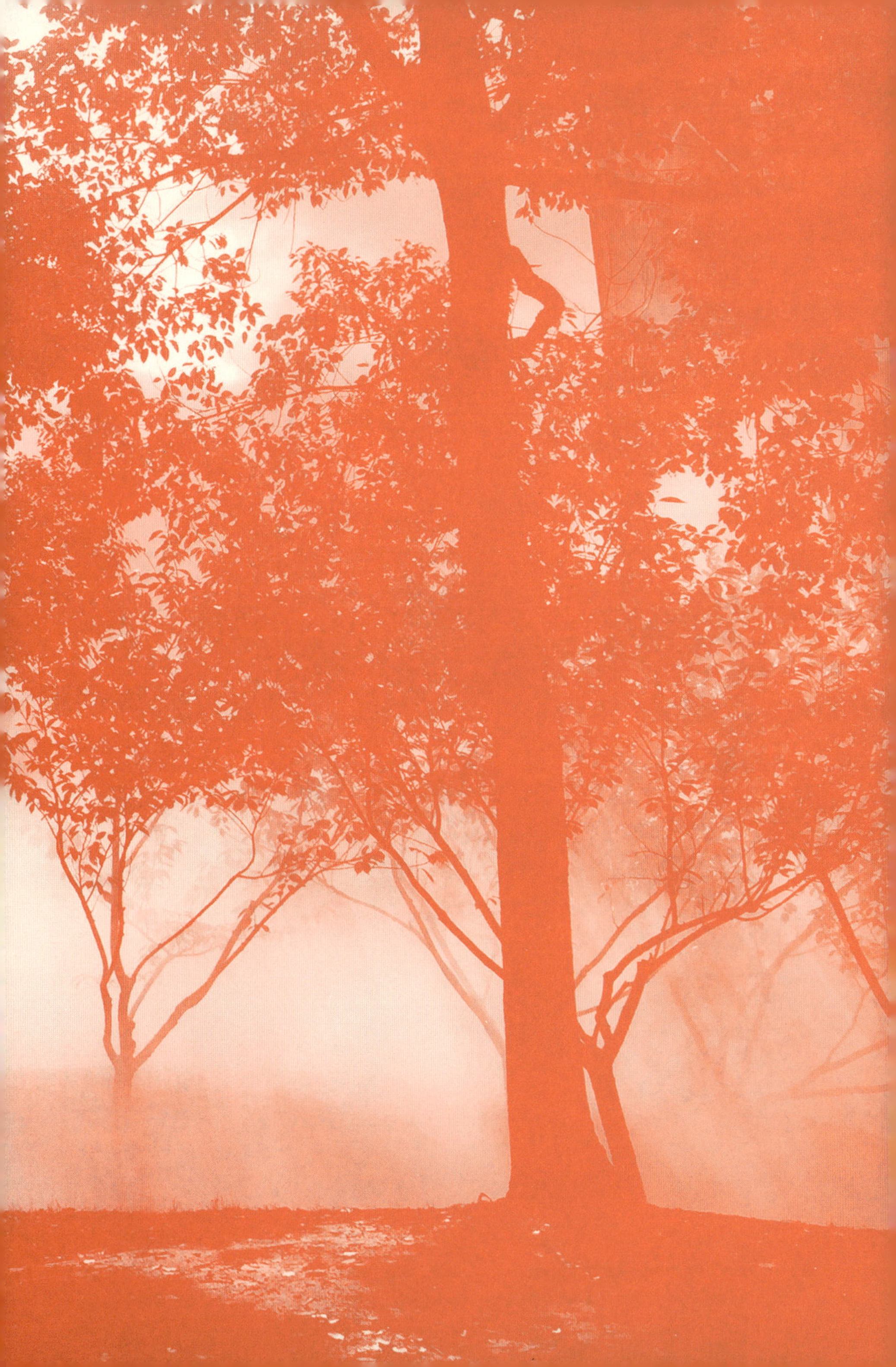

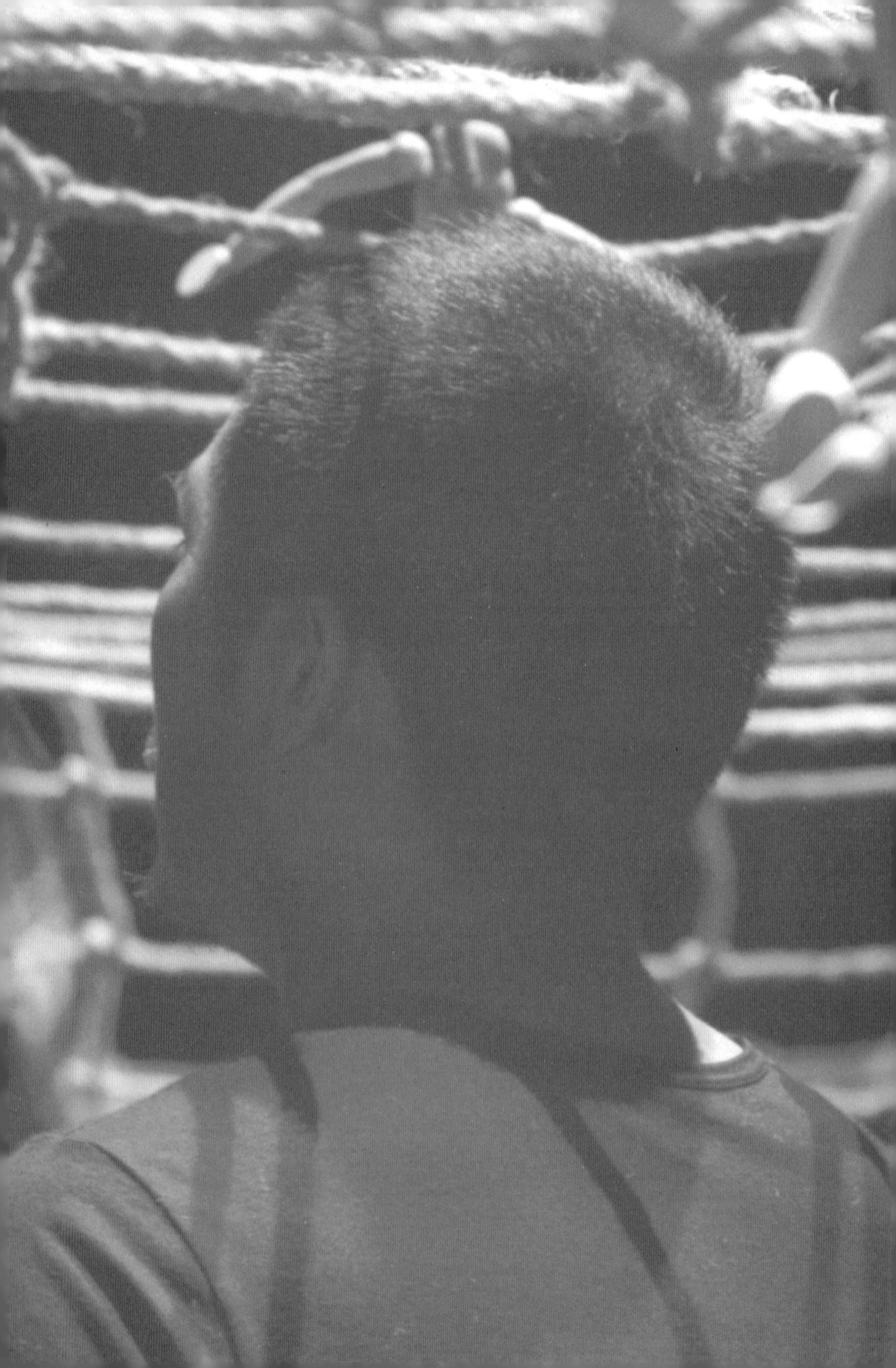

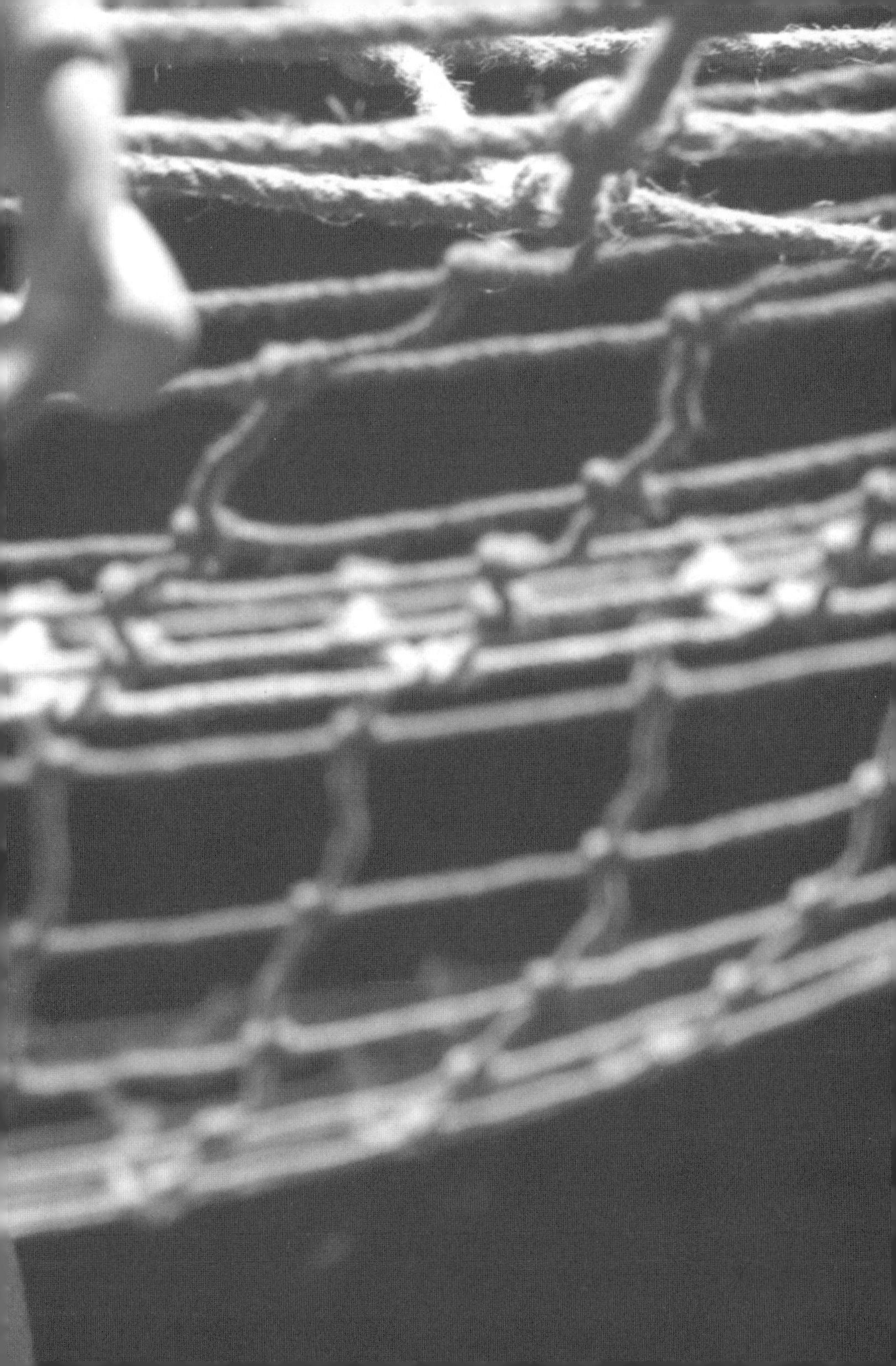

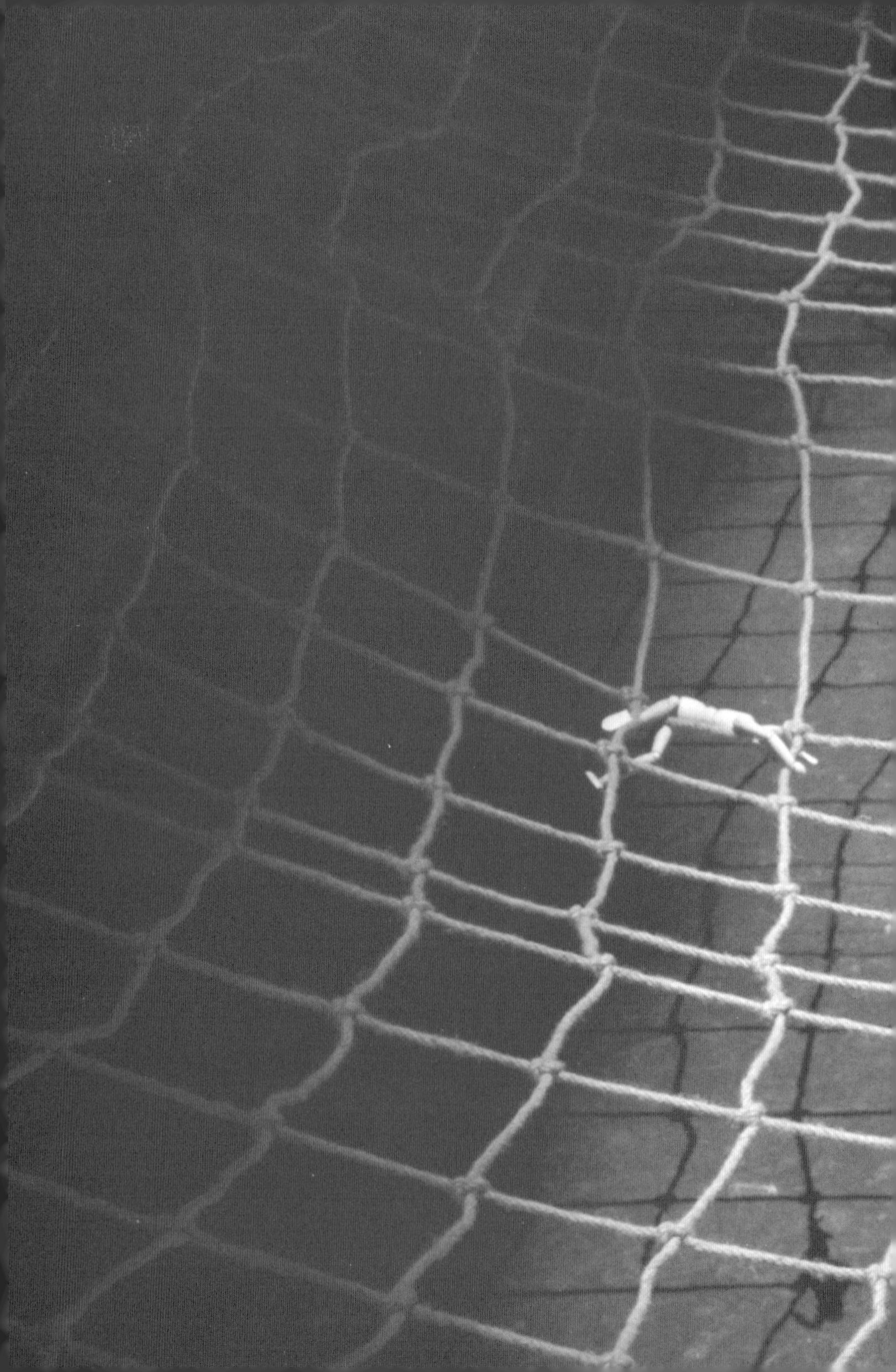

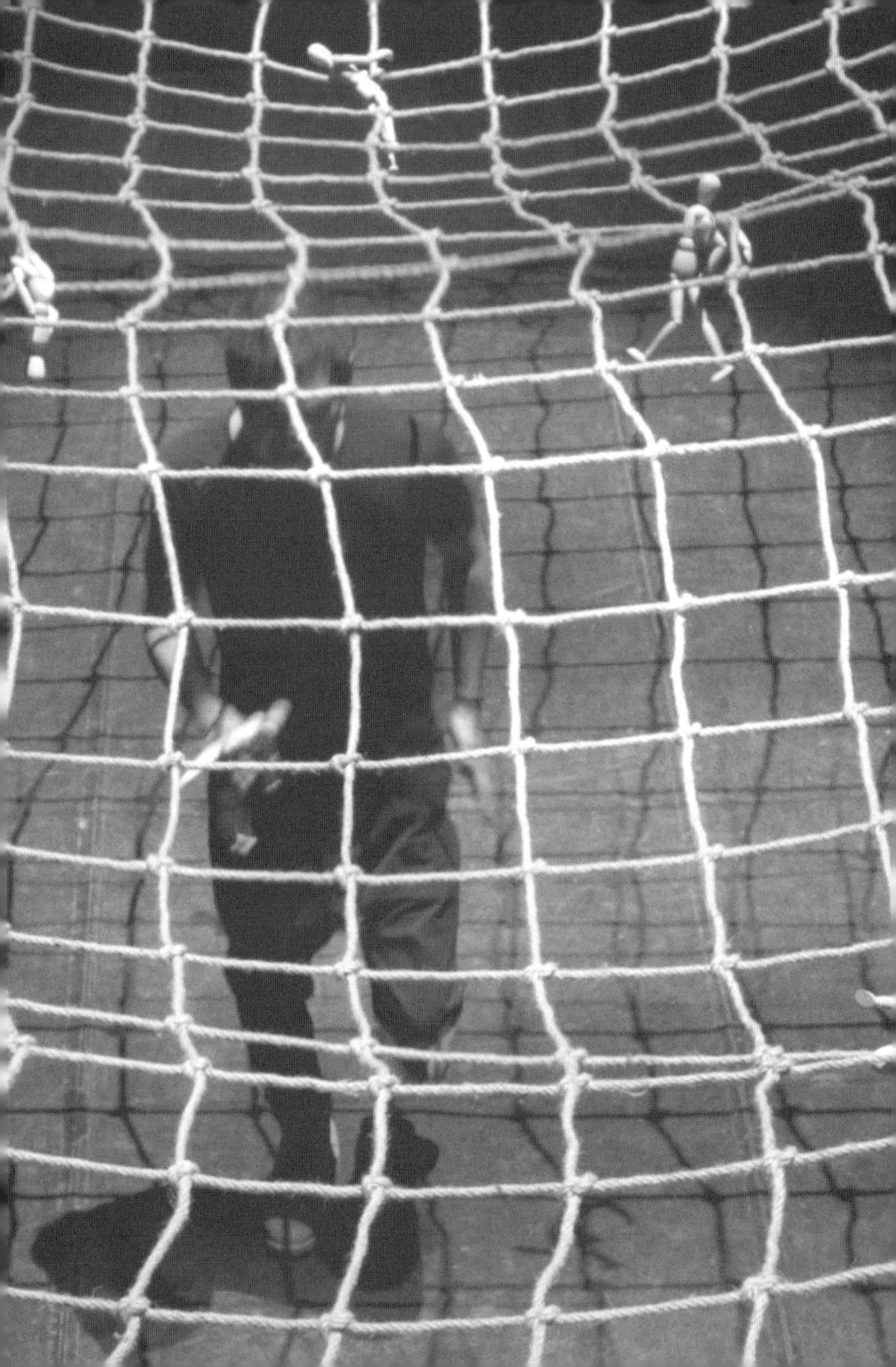

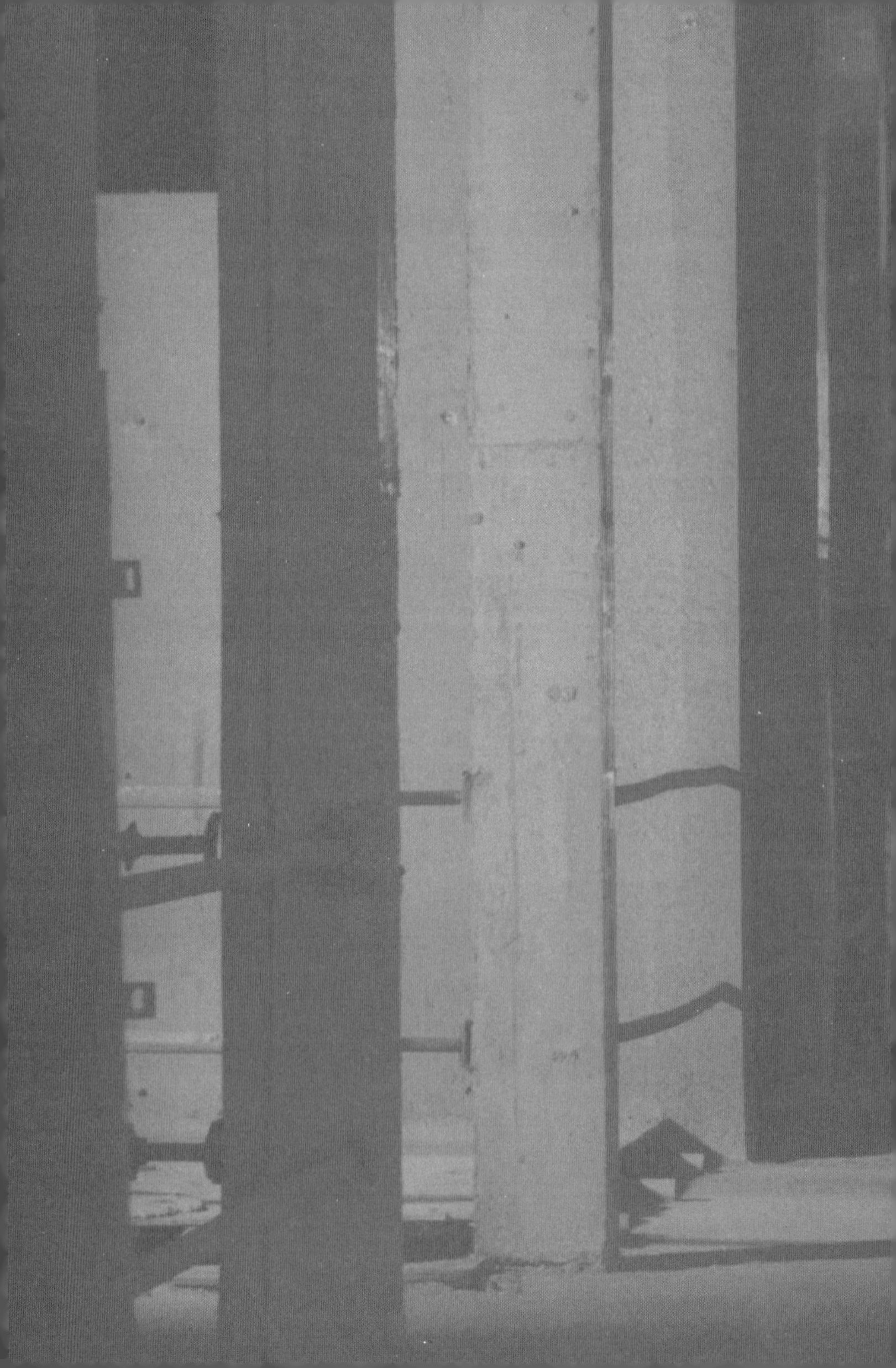

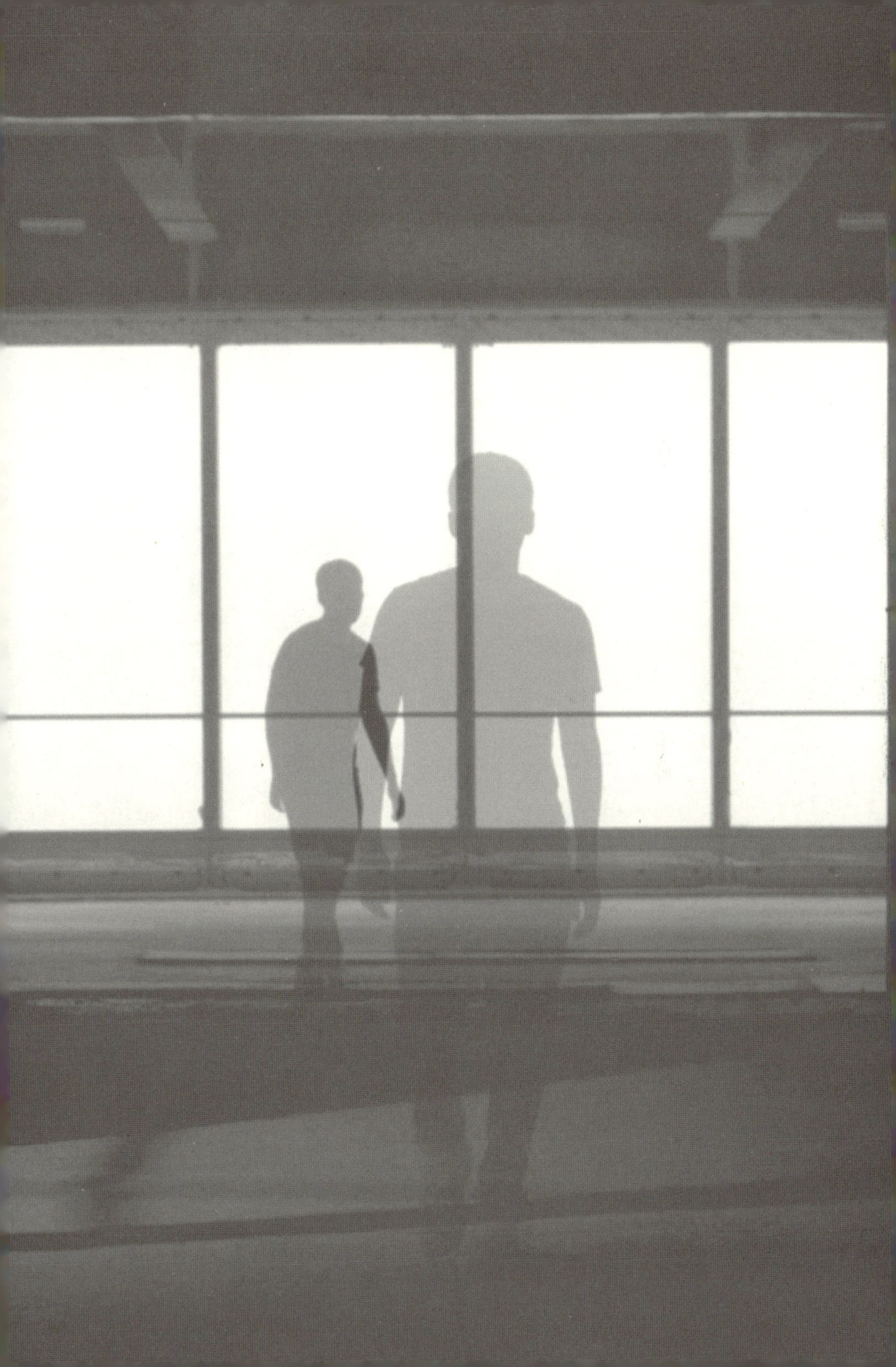

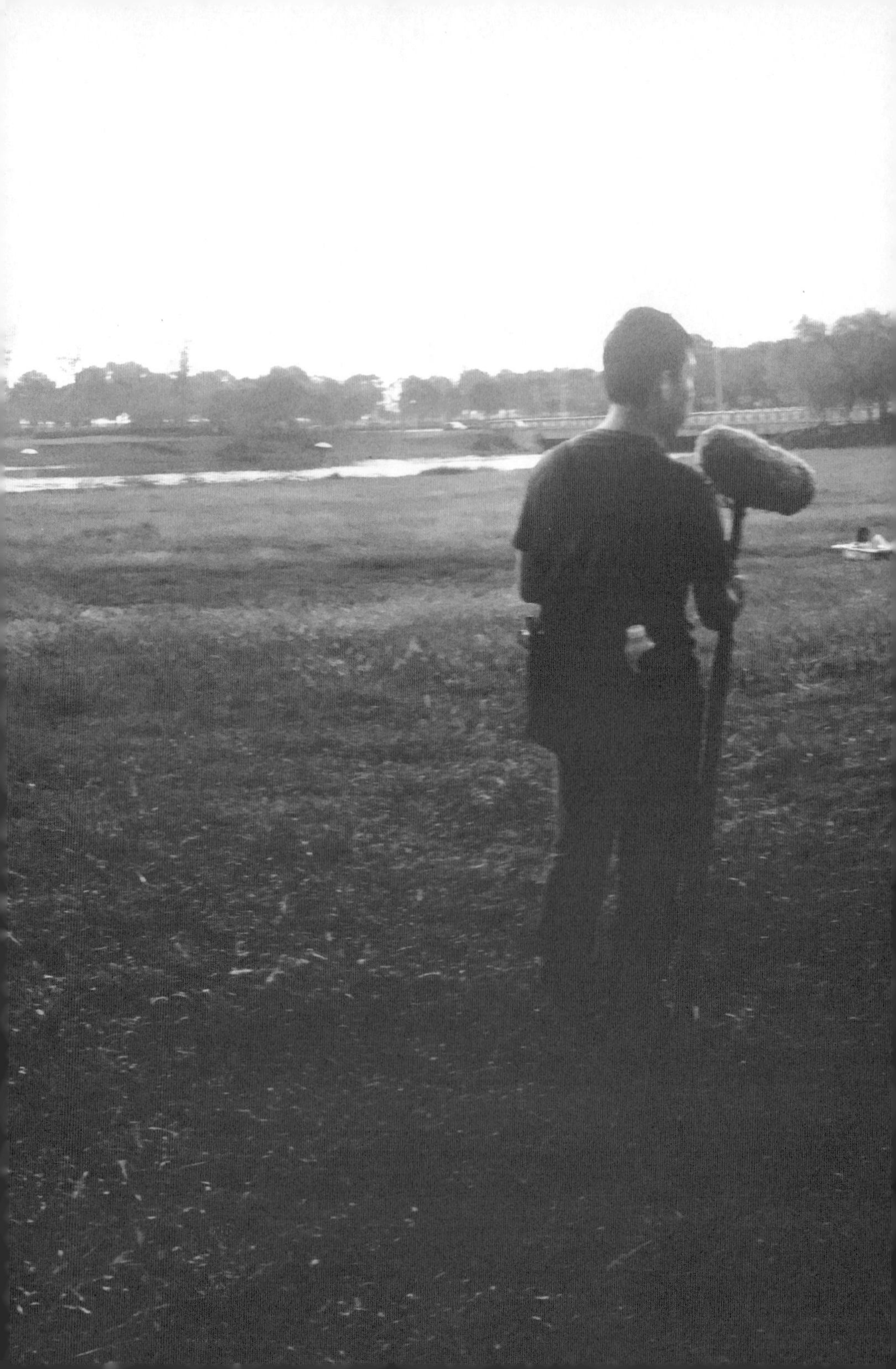

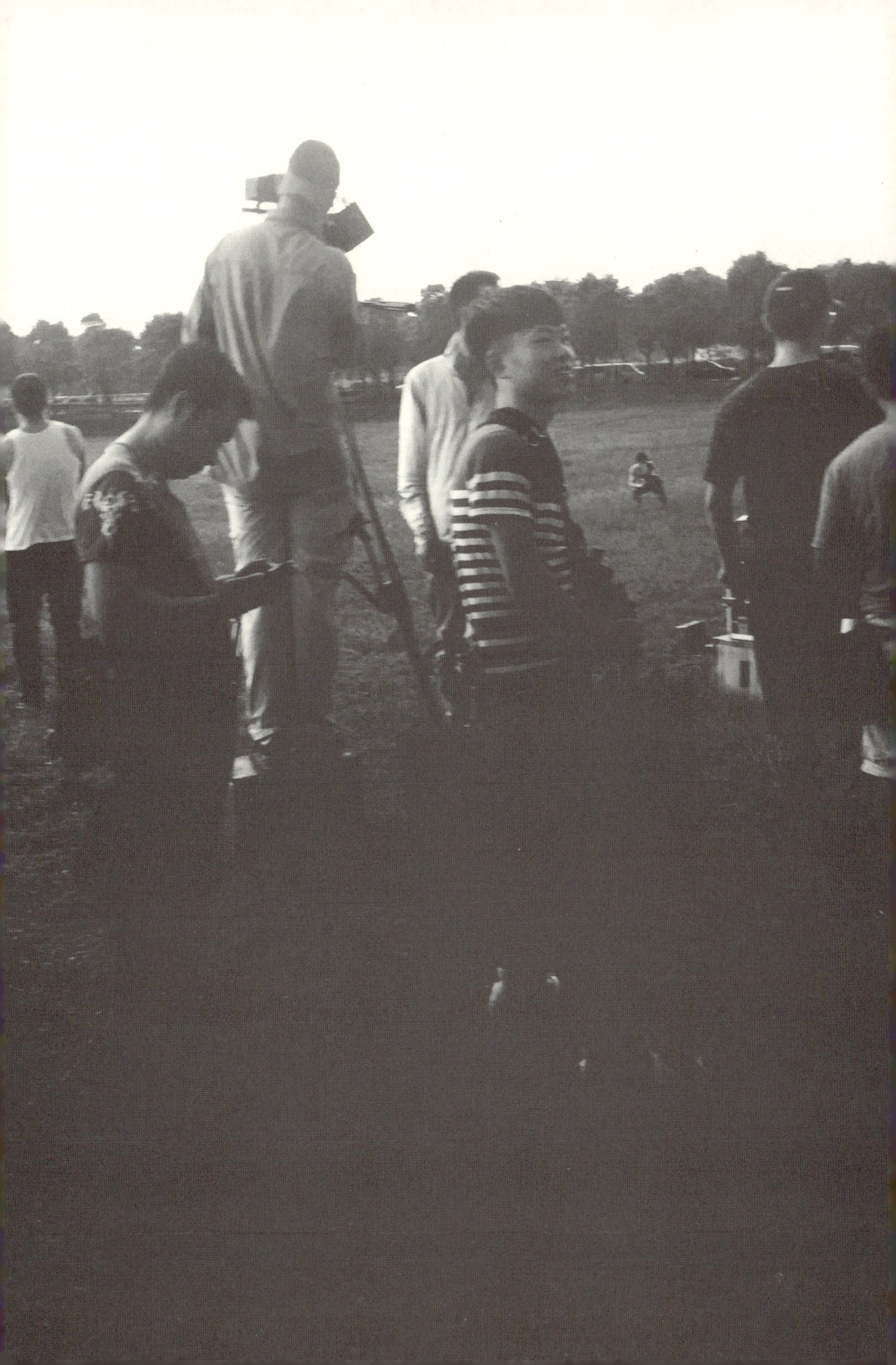

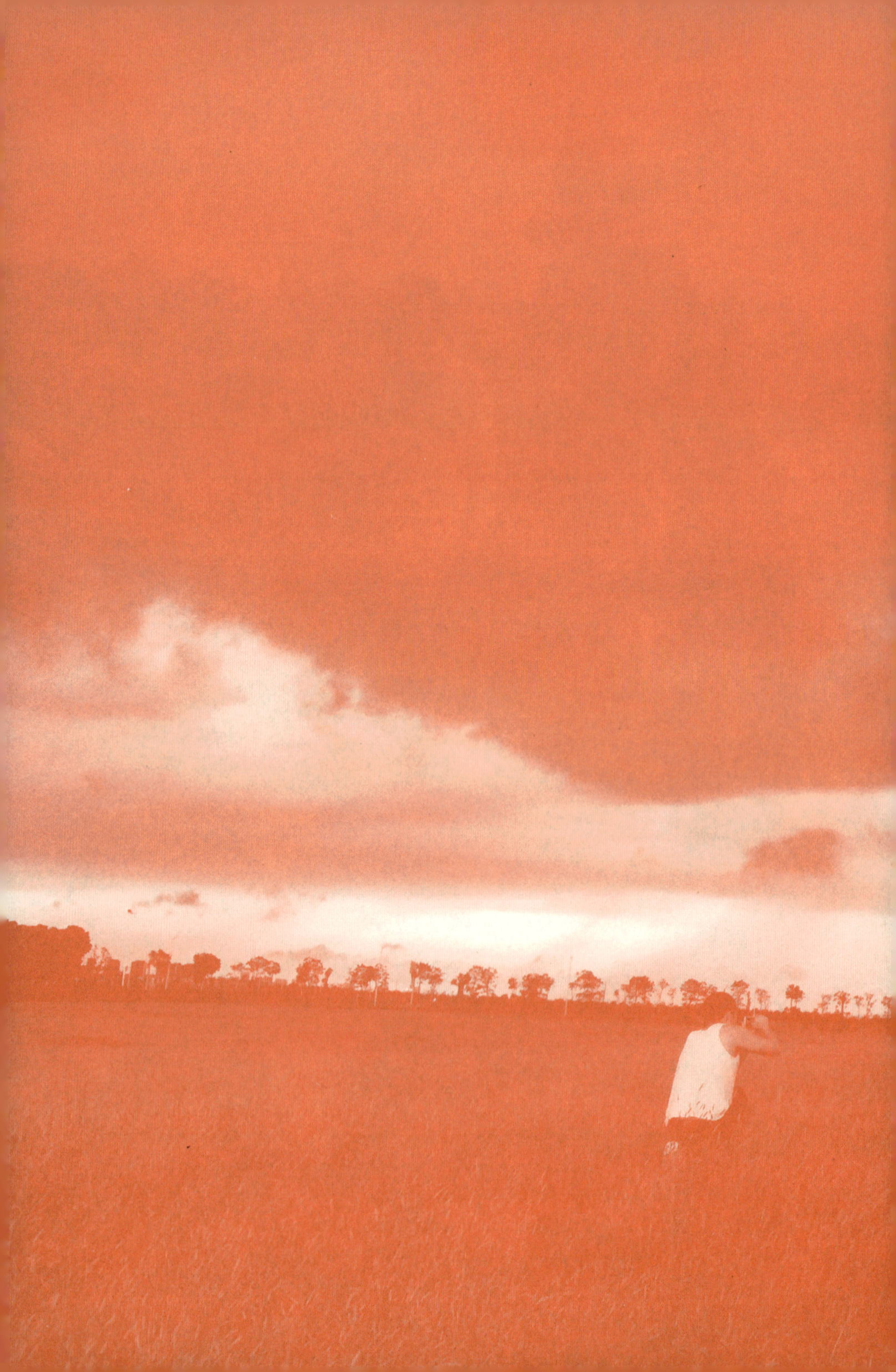

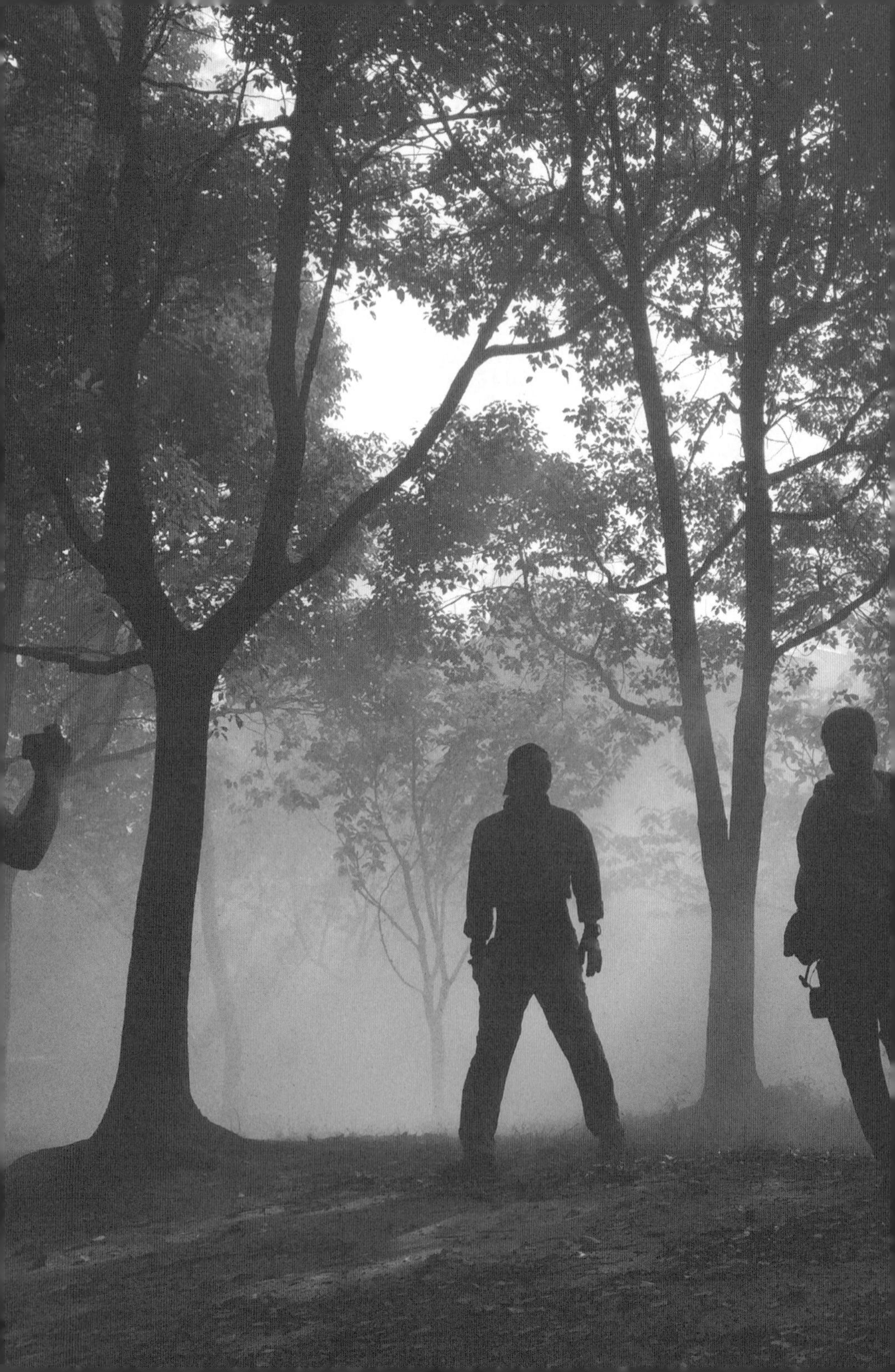

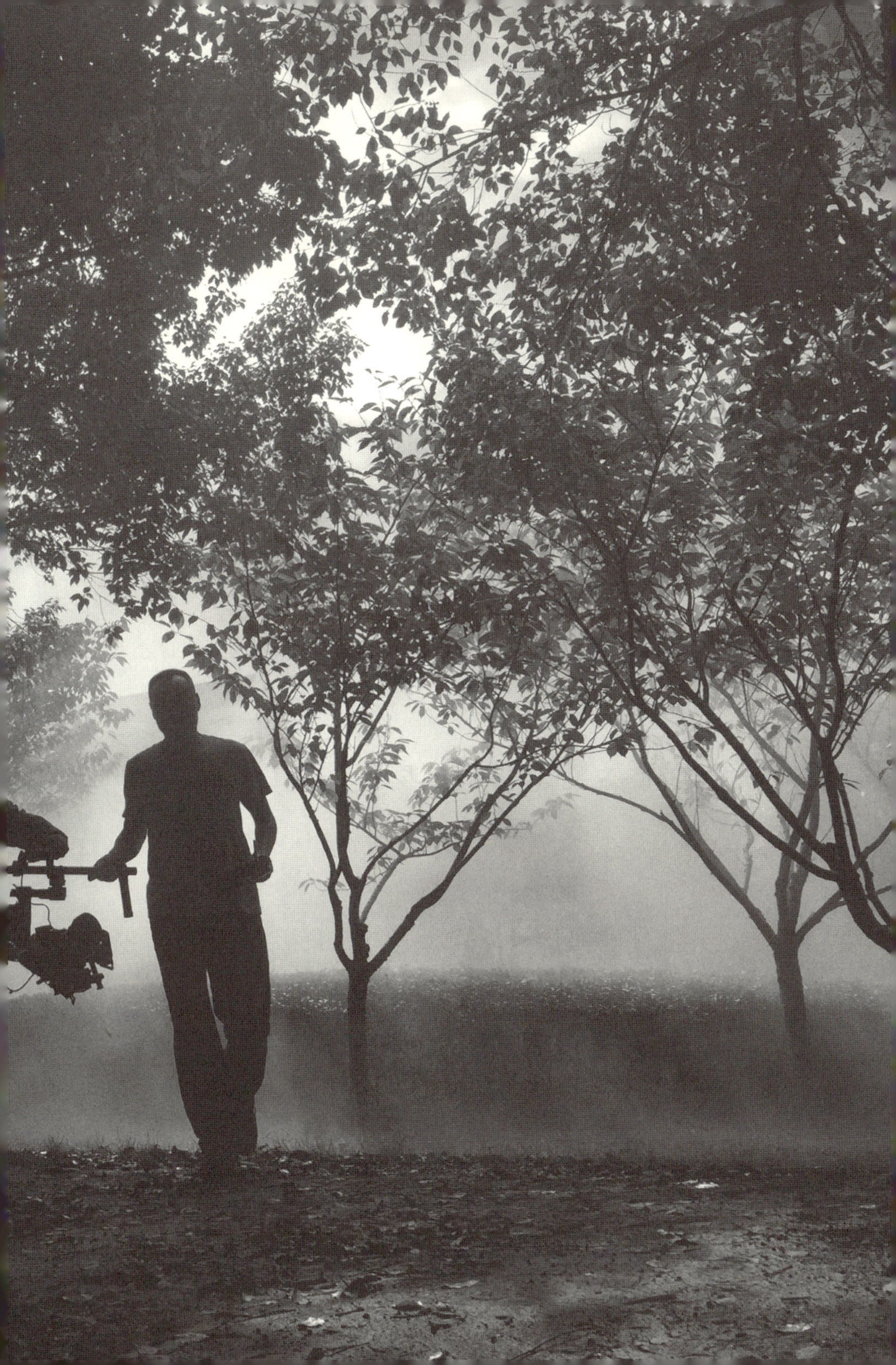

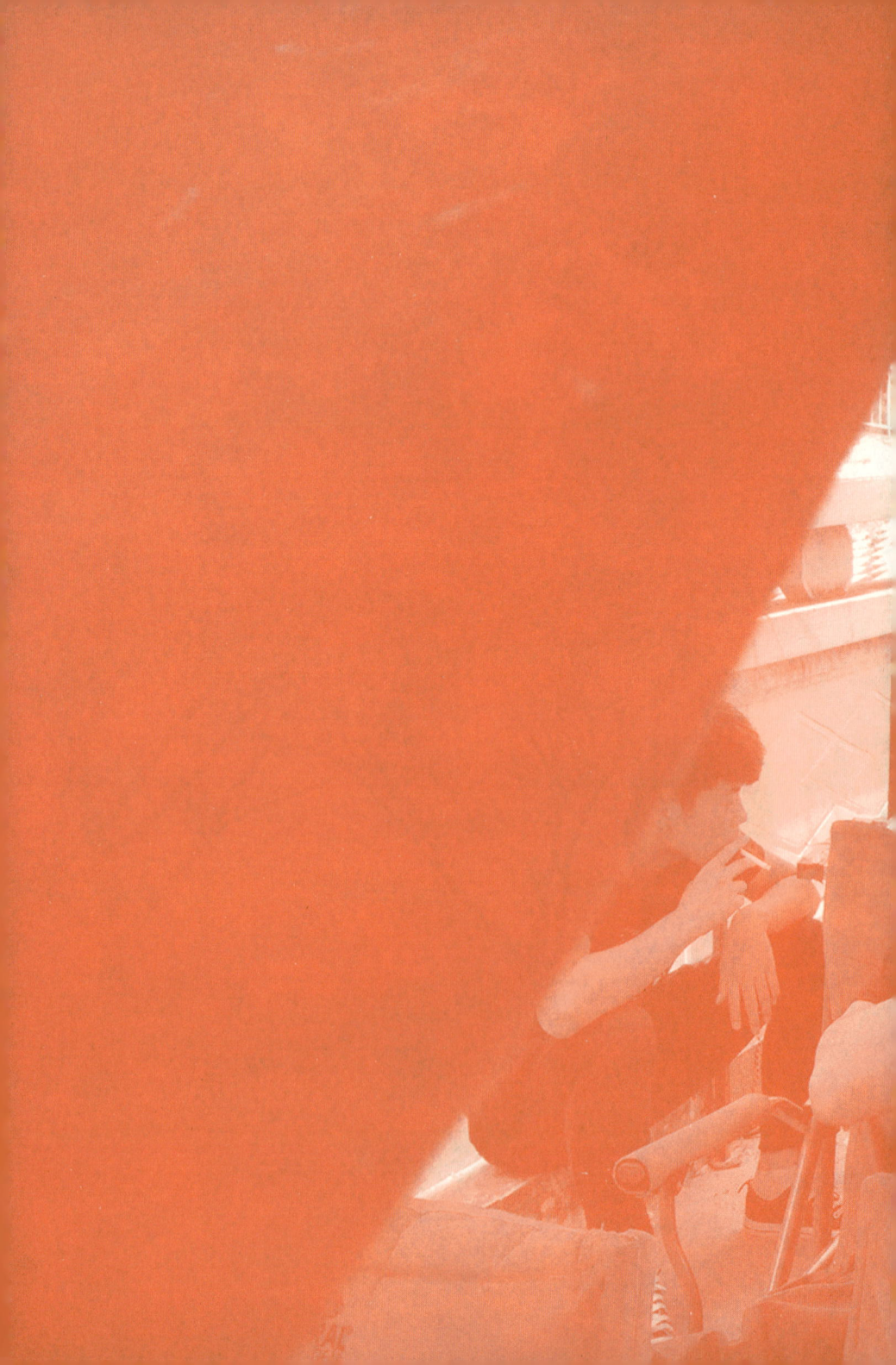

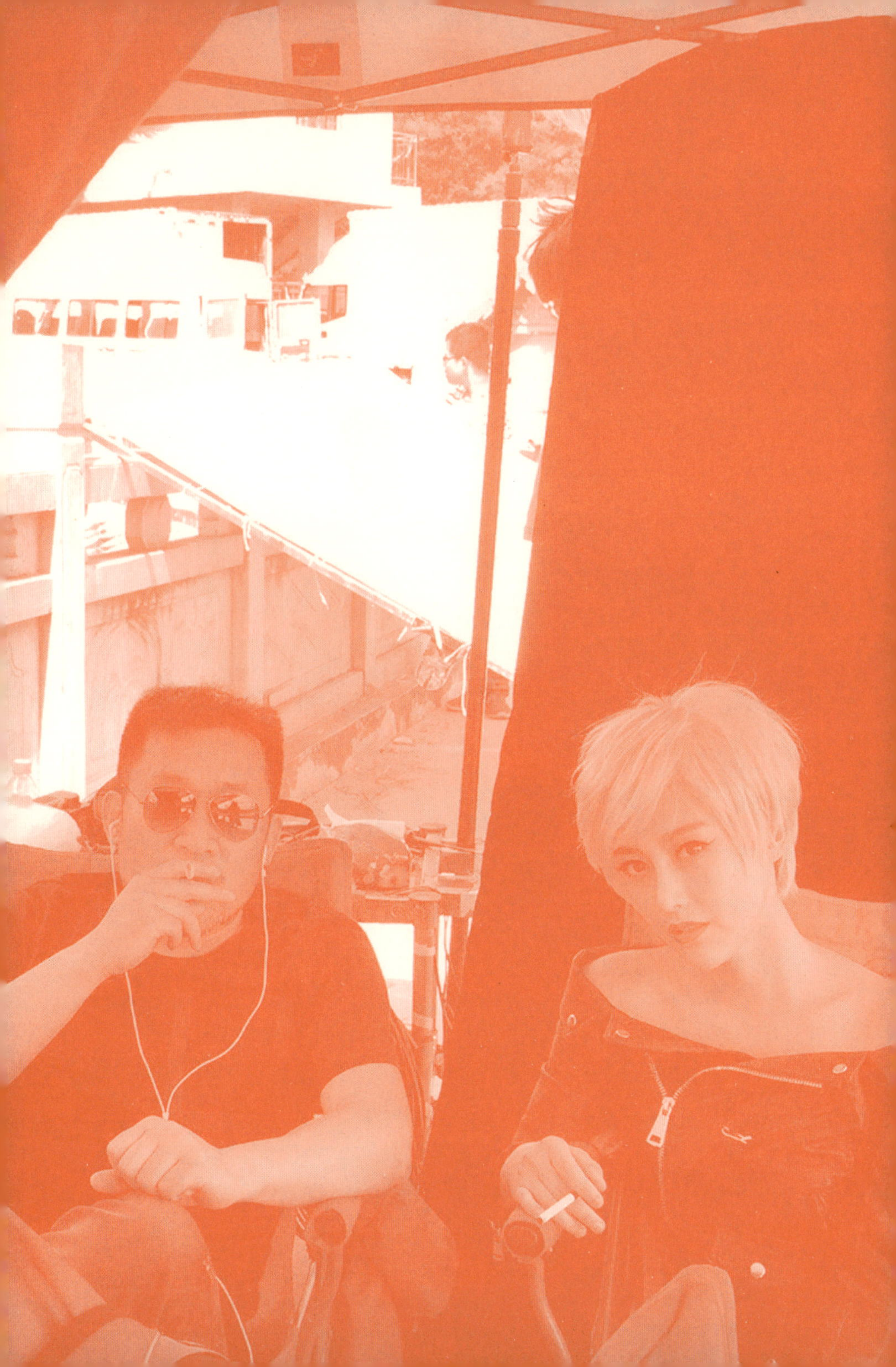

If The Wheat Dies

Magicicada

周期蝉

Translated by

Suzanne Zheng
Jeffrey Twitchell-Waas
Paul Manfredi

If the Wheat Dies

Preface

A type of cicadas in North America live underground for 17 years before they develop into their mature forms with wings, thus they're called Periodical Cicadas. After they stay underground for 17 years, they come to the surface, climb onto a tree, shed exoskeleton and then mate. The male cicadas die right after mating and the female cicadas die after producing eggs. Scientists' explanation of such a unique life style of periodical cicadas is that they have developed this lengthy and furtive life cycle in order to avoid invasion by predators and continue the species safely.

题记

北美洲一种穴居十七年才能化羽而出的蝉，别称"周期蝉"。它们在地底蛰伏十七年始出，尔后附上树枝蜕皮，然后交配。雄蝉交配后即死去，母蝉亦于产卵后死。科学家解释，十七年蝉的这种奇特生活方式，为的是避免天敌的侵害并安全延续种群，因而演化出一个漫长而隐秘的生命周期。

Oh, My Heart of Hearts

I disclose several small secrets of mine.

First, I seldom sleep. That is to say I have cut off a part of time being dead.

Second, I like paper, especially the sanitary bags on the airplane. I never threw up.

Third, I'm also fond of Mona Lisa. But she is the Mona Lisa asleep.

Fourth, I pay attention to a performance about a magicicada, because it presents to people all sorts of movements and vibrations around them.

Fifth, when I get into the elevator, I have an expectation to meet Tofu. Tofu is the dog that lives on the 22th floor.

Very well. Five secrets are disclosed.
I won't say any more.

哦，内心

我透露我的几个小秘密。

第1，我很少睡觉。也就是说我扣去了一部分我死去的时间。

第2，我喜欢纸，尤其喜欢飞机上的清洁袋。我没有吐过。

第3，我还喜欢蒙娜丽莎。但她是睡着的蒙娜丽莎。

第4，我注意一个关于周期蝉的表演，因为它向人们展示身边的各种运动和震动。

第5，我进电梯时有一个期待，就是遇见豆腐。豆腐是22楼那只狗的名字。

好。已经透露了五个。

其他不说了。

Irony

I crawl

down to the underground

to see the trees' roots

This scene, you call it a cross section.

The trees are thriving on the ground

the trees are more thriving under the ground.

But I just prefer crawling down to the underground

to watch the running dogs and the teeth-and-claws

to watch how the wood flatter each other

guarding earth regardless of death

In the underground, you also see other scenes.

It's a wooden palace under the ground. In the palace,

naturally, there are

wooden men.

I take a count today. One, two, three, four

at least seven or eight wooden men are there.

The wooden men don't have faces, which you surely didn't expect.

Some of them are covered by white paper

some are wrapped in red cloth

some are oil-painted or

plastered with lime

You look at a cross section,

in the intellectuals' view, of course you won't see a thing.

Can the wooden men run under the ground?

Can the wooden men fly under the ground?

Do the wooden men cosplay as the Ironman?

Do the wooden men cosplay as the Spiderman too?

What on earth are these questions?

Check out the underground on your own.

But I shall tell you in advance, there's a door to the underground.

Half of it

is sealed tight by darkness.

反讽

我尝试着

爬到地底下去

看树的根

这场景，就是你说的横截面。

地上的树茂盛地开着

地下的树根更茂盛地开着

但我就喜欢爬到地底下去，

看走狗、看爪牙

看木头如何互相巴结

死守着泥土

到地下，你也会看到其他的景象

地下是个木头的宫殿，宫殿里自然有：

木头人。

今天我数了数，一个、两个、三个、四个

木头人起码也有七八个。

木头人没有脸,你肯定没有想到。
他们有被白纸罩住的,
有被红布罩住的,
也有被油漆刷过的抑或
被石灰,刷过的

你看一个横截面,这是
知识分子的看法,当然就无法看到。

"那么木头人有在地下疾走的吗?"
"那么木头人有在地下飞翔的吗?"
"木头人装钢铁侠吗?"
"木头人也装蝙蝠侠吗?"

这都是些什么问题啊?
你们也爬到地下看看。

只是我先告诉你,地下有一门,半扇
已被黑紧紧封住。

The Parakeet by Water

Back to table

watch the bright twilight in the sky from window.

Watch flame beyond the trauma.

A naked kid drives his parakeet

as high as above roofs, back to water bank.

An azure saw makes noise solely

a piece of skull is under the hand

only I hear its unhappy voice

The fire is lit. Drive the parakeet

onto the fire. "Just no!"

The bird is as tough as the master.

The kid walks back. His face, straight like a line of

words,

is greener than the flame tip.

Back to table

watch the bright twilight in the sky from window.

Watch flame beyond the trauma.

If The Wheat Dies

Grass stalks in fall approach me

arrived another death notice.

A lady is peeling lilies and weeping silently,

her silver snake hair astonished me.

The kid continues walking,

burnt clothes are torn up on the lake

and then all scattered.

A coffin was delivered to the bottom of water.

Fish is on tree.

The sinful parakeet has no place to hide.

The faint glow of the lake

is like greenish lips of a black face.

A crowd gathers around fighting roosters.

A grandmother imagines cavalrymen in the warring age.

A pitch of water, a small mare

the woman's face glistens with weird dews.

The kid continues walking

the smell of chicken dung makes him frown.

He turns around

and disappears instantly.

Back to table

watch the bright twilight in the sky from window.

Watch flame beyond the trauma.

The maid in the paintings is in the south

her five fingers are piercing like sharpen pencils

I can only see its gradually-blackening nails

under is a mirror

a gilt water basin.

She will do toilet for the dead.

It's a romance in the South

just like a wedding banquet.

Flute men, carrying parakeets

look for food and poems.

The kid continues walking

he follows the sound of water stirred by

China tree, to tell directions.

(Who is it?

He wears a crown made of golden paper. With soap bubbles,

fish scales are pasted on the crown.

He is deaf. He also squinted his eyes, not able

to see much of other things anymore.)

On the lake,

just by a scarlet nickel,

the thieves can find furies in the lake.

The lake is like a dying lung of an alligator

and I simply breathe the dampness of its chest

the paper and the wood on me make risky vibration.

A rock died on a plain boulevard.

A cart of grass stalks produced green smoke of fire.

Snakes and snake hunters are all on the boulevards.

The lake is already extinguished.

The kid

continues walking.

He hides his breath

in the woody numbness. A dim light

is reflected on half of his face, which is like

a fragment of a ceramic bowl.

The kid continues walking.

His bare feet hit slabs

his toes spit

the parakeet behind him continues shouting shamelessly

"Just no!"

as if a dead chicken were mistakenly

thrown into a stable.

(A horse passes a grassy hillside

just like a sheep passing it

horses have lost their own quality.

A skinny horse

is passing the grassy hillside

it prick its two gentle ears and brings them together

trying to make a knot.

The horse.

An inferior horse of the South

walks back to the stable

more happily than it walks to the hillside.)

Back to table

watch the bright twilight in the sky from the window.

Watch flame beyond the trauma.

The wooden clock on the wall has stopped.

Its brown heart is like a pupil

floating in the hole, detached from the eye socket

in all directions.

It was the only one who heard precisely the kid near water.

The fire touches his hair in the blink of an eye

emitting a rotten smell.

The fire is lit. The wings of the parakeet

turn greener and even purplish.

The kids' four limbs, like wooden clogs

clutch earth. What are caught are the parakeet's

decorative tail feathers and

words.

The swirling treetop sheds cinders.

A skull. A paper mask. A flat body

a calf is ruminating under the light.

Parakeets on the velvet look majestic

and splendorous. Cases with copper hoops

which are coffins, are hidden deep at the bottom of the lake.

The sinful parakeet, the twirling tongue

returns to its root hairs. Sweet words.

connected to water bank forever.

Will catalyze grass and flower stems in the south.

The sinful parakeet. The snake.

"Just no!"

Will not die.

水边鹦鹉

回到桌边

看窗外天边的艳霞。

看伤病以外的火焰。

赤条条的孩子,赶着鹦鹉

已经高过屋顶,回到水边。

瓦蓝的锯条,独自作响

一块颅骨在手下

只有我听到它不够快活的声音。

点火了。赶着鹦鹉

到火上去。"偏不!"

鸟与人一样坚强。

孩子往回走,脸,一字排开

比火焰的边缘更绿。

回到桌边

看窗外天边的艳霞。

看伤病以外的火焰。

秋天的草垛,向我逼近

又传来一位逝者的消息。

剥百合的女子,悄声啜泣

她银色的蛇发,令我十分惊异。

孩子继续行走,

焚毁的衣衫,在湖上

撕碎后又东飘西散。

一具灵柩被深深送入水底。

鱼在树上。

恶鹦鹉已无处可藏。

微薄的湖光

像黑色面孔中粉绿的嘴唇。

人群包围着斗鸡。

祖母想象着战争年代的骑兵。

一罐淡水,一匹小母马

妇人脸上闪着诡异的露珠。

孩子继续行走

鸡粪的气味使他蹙了蹙眉头

他一转身

便已不见

回到桌边

看窗外天边的艳霞。

看伤病以外的火焰。

画上的女奴,她在南方

五指尖锐,如刨光的铅笔

我只看得见它一点点乌黑的指甲

以下是一块镜子

一只饰金的水盆。

她将为逝者梳洗。

情爱,在南方

恰似一场婚宴。

吹笛人携带鹦鹉

找寻吃食和诗篇。

孩子继续行走

他只沿着楝树叶掀起的

水声,辨别方向

  (是谁?

他糊着金纸的王冠。又用皂沫,在

王冠上粘贴鳞片。

他是哑巴。他眯缝着双眼,已不可

能看到其他。)

窃贼,在湖上

一枚血红的镍币,

就能找到湖中的妖怪。

湖仿佛鳄鱼濒死的肺。

而我只是嗅着胸腔的潮湿

纸和木质发出危险的颤栗。

一块石头,死于平坦的大路。

一驾草垛,生出了青烟如火。

蛇和捕蛇人都已到了大路上。

湖,却已熄灭。

孩子

继续行走。

把呼吸隐藏在

麻木里。一片微光

映着他半边脸额宛若

一只瓷碗的残片。

孩子，继续行走。

他的赤脚打在石板上

脚趾吐着唾沫

身后的鹦鹉

继续，无耻地叫喊：

"偏不！"

如同一只死鸡被错误地

投掷在马厩中。

   （马走过草坡正

像羊走过草坡

这是马丧失了自己的品质。

清瘦的马

走过草坡

它把两只柔顺的耳朵

竖起并靠拢着

试图打个花结。

马。

南方的劣马。

走回马厩

比走向草坡更快活。）

回到桌边

看窗外天边的艳霞。

看伤病以外的火焰。

墙上的木钟，早已停止。

棕黑色的心脏，像悬浮在深洞中的

瞳仁，四周不着眼眶。

唯有它准确地听到水边的孩子。

火，一瞬间擦上他的发丝

开始发出一阵腐臭。

点火了，鹦鹉的双翅

绿得发紫。

孩子的四肢木屐一般

抓紧泥土。截获鹦鹉

矫饰的尾羽和

言辞。

旋转的树冠，留下灰烬。

头骨。纸面具。扁平的身体

牛犊反刍于光中。

丝绒上的鹦鹉，显得富丽而

堂皇。铜箍的套盒

那是灵枢，深藏湖底。

恶鹦鹉，翻腾的舌头

返回它的根须。蜜语。

永远连接水边。

催动南方的青草和花茎。

恶鹦鹉。蛇。

"偏不！"

不死。

The Avant-Garde

If I

lost two legs

what would I do

I would still be cheerful

when I were moving on the ground, on the street

I would still be a gentleman and for

beautiful ladies

I would make way

If I lost two legs

I would fly in the sky

yet it might not be elegant, although

I imagined that my

tie was a weather vane

although I imagined

it were guided by the sunshine

If I

lost two legs, in fact

I would just be a wretch

the suitcase would not follow me

the shoes would not follow me

Then I would

mess with my upper body:

I would dye my hair orange

let it look fancy

I would fill my chest with an air

let it show whatever

I would cast humankind deliberately and they

also would not care about my misconduct, understanding

it were a result of my anger.

If I were sent to the hell

I would practice weight lifting

my muscle could obviously be

much stronger.

If I climbed up to the blue sky

I would practice swimming

this swimming pool

would be much higher

than all the seas that

you saw

If I

lost my two legs, I would sit on a boat

I would wait cheerfully for

the death tomorrow.

先锋派

如果我

没有了双腿,我

怎么办

还一副兴高采烈的样子

在地上走,在街道上走

还要像绅士一样为

漂亮的女士

让路

如果我没有了双腿

那我就应该在天上飞

但这并不优雅,虽然

我想象了我的

领带,它是一个风向标

虽然我想象了

它被阳光牵引

如果我

没有了双腿，实际上

就是一倒霉蛋

旅行箱不跟随我了

鞋也不跟随我了

那么，我就会在

上半身做文章：

我把头发染成橘色

它显得很炫

我为胸脯充满了气体

它也显得，什么

我故意撇下人类，人类

也大人不计小人过，明白

这是我愤怒的结果

我下了地狱

我练举重

我的肌肉明显

更强健了

我上了蓝天

我练游泳

这个游泳池

比你看到的

所有大海

还高

如果我

没有了双腿,我就坐在小船上

兴高采烈地等着

明天的死。

By Rice Straws

This is morning.

Three people are sitting around spring straws.

One of them is singing a Czech song:

"Damp straws,"

"Damp straws,"

He is covering his body

with damp straws, stalk by stalk.

Another person of less than twenty years old

delicate and pretty, talks to himself:

"If I love a woman

marry her

if I love a woman

marry her not

just bask straws with her

here, the air

is fragrant and clear."

"Whereas I—," the third person

is more resolute:

"Will go far. Sit in a carriage

turn at a high point.

Gold paves the road.

What wonderful days

even if

they are like dews!"

稻草旁

这是早晨。

三个人围着春天的稻草。

一个人哼着捷克的歌曲

"潮湿的稻草",

"潮湿的稻草",

他让潮湿的稻草

一根根覆盖在身上;

另一个人,二十岁不到

自言自语,清秀漂亮:

"假如爱一个女人,娶她做妻子

假如爱一个女人,不娶她做妻子

只要我们一起晒稻草

这里的空气清新又芳香";

"而我——"

第三个人更加果断:

"到远处去。坐上马车。

在一个高处转弯。

黄金像稻草铺路。

美妙的日子啊,哪怕是

露水一样的时光!"

White Sand Spring 1

A girl wanted to play cool, I think

in order to play cool, she painted her whole body with

waves, branches and clouds

Waves were at the bottom,

branches in the middle

the clouds, of course, on the top

This girl became a bottle

her skin a coat.

When winter came, she was frozen

But got taller gradually

even two times taller than

she had been before. Many people

Must reach hands very high

to touch her

tummy

白沙泉 1

有个女孩儿为了扮酷我想

她是为了扮酷她把整个身体画满了

水浪、树枝和云彩

水浪是在下面的

树枝在中间

当然云彩就在上面了

女孩儿成了一个瓶

她皮肤的部分成了一个外套

冬天到的时候女孩儿结成冰了

但是渐渐地她越长越高

比原来的她自己也高出了

两倍。许多人

现在要高高地伸长手

才能摸到她的

肚皮。

White Sand Spring 2

Still this girl, she wanted to pose as a grown-up, I think

in order to pose as a grown-up, this girl decided

to have a meditation

Her meditation didn't have any purpose, but she made

the request that she would spend more than six months

for the meditation

The adults don't get it at all, but for sure it is

horrible. In six months, flowers shall bloom several

rounds

nothing won't wither

Nevertheless they could do nothing but let her meditate

When she meditate, they can't wake her up even by

pouring water on her

which somebody tried

Later they tried another trick. They blended the water

into a spunk-water and splashed it on her

then she woke up.

白沙泉 2

还是这个女孩儿为了装大人我想

她是为了装大人她决定

要做一次冥想

她的冥想没有目的她只提出

一个要求,要求要花六个月以上的

时间来冥想

大人们百思不得其解想想也是

可怕的。六个月可能花儿也开了好几批了

不信没有不枯萎的

然而人们只能让她冥想

她冥想时水都泼不醒她

有人试过

后来人们又试了一招　当把水

调成仙水后再泼她

她就醒了。

Maize (Jade Rice) Master

Maize, a gamboge silhouette.

Marching. White teeth. Her. She lets her two ears,

she, takes the lead. He lets her two ears

stand straight in vermilion. Like bunny's ears.

Sharp tenderness. The circle

warm.

Bean petals. On a coconut tree.

Her eye. A fish.

Fish eye. On which brown twigs dangle.

Also like. A fish bone bearing green leaves.

She. Can fly.

Can swim.

Can eat.

Her hand.

Seems like a drummer.

If The Wheat Dies

Peng, peng, peng, ka peng

Cow's tongue. Lapping the flame tip.
Her eye. It's also
cow's eye.

Leave branches in dream, steel wires
by which the fruit is twisted tight.
Vibrating.

Maize. Marching.
Coral-shaped hair ornament. Wraps
the body. Face. Fair,
fair white. Fairly white to be jade rice.
Marching and advancing.

The root of the coconut tree. Simple.
Like a chicken feet.
The coconut tree. Oh-Jee.
Rambles.
Extremely Resembles.

Maize. A duck in the green.

Also with pears. Duck pears.

Hidden in the pears (li) core is your gift

" 离 "(li). Her figure.

Also seems a plow (li).

She. Can plant

can harvest.

Can sing. Most of the singing

is eaten.

Delis, delis.

Lightens the sheep:

"You guys are so cold, so — cold!"

A Japanese shoe

in eggshell blue.

Maize. Marching.

She looks lost. Arms

seem loosened braids. Strayed.

The fiddle fretboard plays the fool. A grape

posed as a lotus.

Prance,

dance,

bare feet,

kick feet,

Music stand. A tool of bread earning.

Foodstuff is on the floor. Flour. White.

Pancake. Yellow.

Bare feet. Like a broom,

clung with beard hairs.

Party.

Red and Purple.

Blossomed flower petals.

Contemplating.

Jade. Waiting for you. Greeting you.

Receiving you.

Jade and rice,

big and small,

red and green,

wheels

Wind leaves. Decorate your body with it.

The chick. Rest it on your chest.

The beak is pointed at you.

Maize.

Like a turtle.

The four limbs on the ground.

A surrendered toy.

The turtles head. "M"

Hands in hands.

Peace, branch.

And wings. Unfolded folding fan.

As cordial as bird's bill. In which the human body wanders.

Duck web.

Jade.

Jade rice. Has seven fingers.

Nails are like pine needles.

Their sting hurts to your heart.

The head-up bird

eating the fish.

Fish eye. Jade rice.

Her feet, in the copper basin.

The water splash, like waves.

Her hands, also seem

chicken wings roused cockscomb.

A whole scene, flame red.

Surreal.

A red flag was planted on the hill.

Jade rice. She. Can bloom.

Can fall.

Can intoxicate.

Cherry blossom intoxicated rose.

Jade rice. Trumpeter.

Blowing piccolo. Sloping shoulder (jian).

Playing hand drum. Sharp (jian) fingers.

Peng, peng, peng, peng up dirts.

Strawberry cake

well-liked.

Her hand. Writes characters.

Her nose. Red character " 山 ".

Her mouth. Green water.

Like an otter. Stand up.
Kissed by her.
She's kissed. A halo
surrounds at the back.

The razor takes a break.
Circus arena in a cave.
Mist grows. Recall
recalling.

Maize.
Spider. Golden silk web.
Three lines of teeth. Two on the right.
Suona horn.
Happy mouth.

Tea cup. Her.

Her.

She. Can silver (yin).

Can drink (yin).

Both cheeks are pasted with green grass.

Her.

She. In the colorful check

walks a horse. The horse's hooves tread

on the "gentleman-sheep" (qun) at home,

Skirt (qun).

Collectively(qun) live.

Tiny hooves.

Big world.

Sir turns head for little cousin-brother.

Jade rice. Her hand. Drummer.

Snickers. Snicker flops finger.

Chips incisor.

Peng, peng, peng. Ka peng.

"Giddyup!"

Rooster holds a chicken coop

catching jade rice

Jade rice rides water buffalo,

looking for rooster.

About children's opera.

Jade rice. Her hand

like fabric. Sews your colorful suits.

Too many to wear. Thick papers.

A tool for pasting and painting.

Singing.

Chess-playing.

Red tassels bloomed on iron helmet.

A paper boat arrived in Norway.

Jade rice. Her hand. Holds the spear tight.

"Go!" The governor falls in water.

Maize.

Marching.

Grass.

Half cup.

"土"."皮"."鱼".

Goldfish.

Swimming in the deep green. Red light like a coal fire.

Goldfish.

Golden skin fish. Skin Golden (pijin).

Fart Goblin (pijin).

Chasing jade rice.

Jade Scent. Jade Flower. Jade Petal. Jade Tinkling. Jade.

Jade Rice. Her hand. Drummer.

Cut through your mountain.

The surrendered eagle. Seems a girl.

Jade Rice. Her hand. Drummer.

Seven fingers.

Sharp fingers.

Purple tips.

Peng. Peng. Peng. Ka peng.

She. Can fly.

Can drink. The tree top is as if a mushroom lightens up heaven above and under.

玉米师傅

玉米，藤黄的侧影。

行进。白牙。她。她把她的双耳，

她，为首。他把她的双耳

直立在朱红中。像兔耳。

尖利的温柔。圆形

温暖。

豆瓣。椰树上。

她的眼睛。鱼。

鱼眼。悬挂着褐色的枝条。

又像。一根鱼骨支持着绿叶。

她。会飞。

会游。

会吃。

她的手。

像鼓手。

蓬，蓬，蓬，卡蓬

牛舌头。舔着火苗。
她的眼睛。又即，
牛眼。

梦中的枝叶，被钢丝
拧紧的果实。
震动。

玉米。行进。
珊瑚样的发饰。包围住
人。脸。白色，
白色。洁白到玉米。
行和进。

椰树的树根。简练。
像鸡爪。
椰树。耶书
向。
至像。

玉米。绿色中的鸭子

也和梨。鸭梨。

梨核中躲藏着你的才智

"离"。她的轮廓

又像"犁"。

她。会种

会收。

会歌。歌的大半

已被吃去。

冷食，冷食

羊照亮：

"你们真冷、真冷啊！"

一只日本鞋

在蛋清之中

玉米。行进。

她惘然着。手臂

仿佛松散的发辫。披散

琴把发傻,装扮着

青莲的葡萄。

跳舞,

舞蹈,

赤脚,

踢脚,

乐谱架。吃饭的利器。

粮食满地。面粉。白。

面饼。黄。

赤着的脚。似扫帚,

沾着胡须。

节日。

红紫。

展开的花瓣。

沉思。

玉。迎候你。迎你。

接你。

玉米，

大小，

红绿，

轮子

把风的叶子。饰上你身体。

鸡雏。歇上你胸脯。

小嘴对你。

玉米。

像龟。

四肢着地。

投降的玩具。

龟首。"M"。

手拉手。

和平，与枝叶

与翅膀。打开的折扇。
亲切如鸟喙。人体于其中
漫游。

蹼。

玉。

玉米。长着七指。
指甲如松针
刺得你心疼

回头的鸟
吃着鱼。

鱼眼。玉米
她的脚,在铜盆里
水花,像波浪。
她的手,又像,
鸡翅扇起鸡冠。

一片、火红

超现实。

红旗插在山岗。

玉米。她。会开。

会败。

也会醉。

樱花醉蔷薇。

玉米。吹鼓手。

吹短笛。削肩。

打手鼓。肩（尖）指。

蓬，蓬，蓬。蓬起土。

草莓的糕点

畅销。

她的手。写字。

她的鼻。红色的"山"字。

她的嘴。绿水。

像一只水獭。竖起。
被她吻。
她被吻。光圈
绕在后背。

停着剃刀。
山凹里的马戏场。
起云雾。想起
想起

玉米。
蜘蛛。金丝的绣网。
三排大牙。右二
唢呐。
高兴的嘴。

茶杯。她。

她。

她。会银。

会饮。

两腮涂上青草。

她。

她。在彩格中

走马。马蹄又踩着

自家的"群",

裙。

群居。

小马蹄。

大天下。

郎顾表弟弟。

玉米。她的手。鼓手。

吃吃笑。笑歪了手指,

掉门齿。

嘣。嘣。嘣。卡嘣。

"驾！"

公鸡押着鸡笼,

捉玉米。

玉米骑上水牛,

找公鸡。

说儿戏。

玉米。她的手

像布匹。缝上你的彩衣。

穿不完。厚纸。

糊绘的工具。

唱歌。

下棋。

红缨开在钢盔。

纸船到了挪威。

玉米。她的手。紧握梭标。

"杀——",总督落下水。

玉米。

行进。

草木。

半杯。

"土"。"皮"。"鱼"。

金鱼。

游在深绿里。红光

像炭火。

金鱼。

金皮鱼。皮金。

屁精。

追逐玉米。

玉芳。玉华。玉英。玉玲。玉

玉米。她的手。鼓手。

劈过你的山峦。

归降的雄鹰。像少女。

玉米。她的手。鼓手。

七指。

肩指。

紫尖。

蓬。蓬。蓬。"卡蓬"。

她。会飞。
会饮。树冠像蘑菇,照亮天上人间。

I'll Write about Autumn Dusk in the Mountains

After getting up in the morning

I went out

I started my day

by describing.

Road is gray

plain is dark

trees are gray and dark.

Among them, only

one tree

is red

I make two

furtive acts

around the tree

I make circles

My body is naked

that's why I got up that early

by being so early,

I wanted to find a miracle

and I did find one.

I sit under the tree

look up at the tree

as if I were looking at

a bird cage

the birds haven't started to sing yet

they are still waking up

that is why their lips appear red

their butts appear red

their toes also appear red

This tree

is also moving

the movement of the light in the morning

forms a stair

there is something strange in the far

that's the woman under star light from last night

a beauty as snow from yesterday evening

becomes as dirty as it can be right now

I care nothing and look at nothing

move forward with my full heart

some gold hunters are along the road now.

They make flying postures

blowing the air to bubbles

gold could be buried deep underground

but the plain persists

it's still a dark

plain

I started to doubt

my acts

it seems that I were looking for a religion

one that was carved on a railing.

My hands rest on it but I

didn't feel any warmth of the morning

its deep color still has

the same temperature as

my naked body

I doubt the language

a simple act

brings suspicion

I try

I pee

I carry an iron pole

jabbing open the sky screen

Sure enough

the morning just started

without going through the day

When I finish this poem

the sky is already gray

already dark

我将写山居秋暝

早晨起来

我出了门

我通过描述

开始了我的一天

道路是灰的

原野是黑的

树木既灰又黑

唯有其中的

一棵树

是红的

我做了两个

蹑手蹑脚的动作

在这棵树前

环绕

我是裸体

所以才起得这么早

出门这么早

我想寻找一个奇迹

这就寻找到了

我坐在树下

抬头仰望着树

像仰望着

鸟笼

鸟还没叫

它们在醒来的过程中

所以嘴唇发红

屁股发红

脚趾也发红

这棵树

还在运动

早晨光线的移动

形成了一个台阶

远处有异物

是昨夜星光下

的女人

昨夜如雪的美

现在也变得

脏脏的

我不管不顾

只管往前走

沿途有一些淘金客了

他们做出飞翔

的姿势

把空气吹得像水泡

金子可能深埋在地中

但是原野坚持着

仍然是黑的

原野

我开始怀疑

我的行为

似乎我在寻找一个宗教

一个刻在栏杆上

的宗教

我手扶了它并没有

感到早晨的暖意

深沉的颜色与

我的裸体仍然是同一个

体温

我怀疑语言

一个简单行为

它会带来悬疑

我试着

我小便

我扛着钢管

去捅破天幕

果然

早晨刚刚开启

没有经过白天

到我写完这首诗

天就灰了

黑了

Control

I set up 4 wedges and

2 stage props

I seldom cared about even numbers, but I just set up

4 wedges and 2 stage props

"Why does it have to be so specific?

You are concerned with relations in this world"

"Yes, I'm concerned with relations"

I have already said it in earnest:

With just a touch, you can hurt me

even waving a club, the world won't hurt me

I have moved love on stage

moved it to the front, hence there are

4 wedges and 2 stage props

car is on hillside

cows come to plain

for love, I have preset color green

in the background, I can also set up

snow mountains, fir trees and log cabin

Yippee! I'm a dark director

but I'm covered with beard today, so I can write the poem

more abstractly

Only 2 props are available to you

4 wedges to pass

"If you want to be in love then you must fall"

"If you want to be in love then you must fall"

When the music is on,

you have to get on stage.

No matter you have memorized or not

the 4 wedges. After getting on the stage, you just have to use

the 1st prop.

支配

设置了四个环节和

两个道具

我很少关注偶数,但就设置了

四个环节和两个道具

"为何如此具象?

你一定在关注这个世界的关系"

"是的,我在关注关系"

我刚才认真说了:

你稍稍一下,就是伤害我

世界纵使挥舞了大棒,也不伤害我

我把爱,搬到了舞台上

搬到面前,这才有了

四个环节和

两个道具

汽车开到山坡上

奶牛来到平原

我为爱预设了绿色

背景上,我还可以安排上

雪山、塔松、小木屋

呵呵,我是黑色的导演啊,

但今天,我贴上了胡须,我就能把诗

写得抽象些

只给了你两个道具

必须经过四个环节

　"你要恋爱就必须要谈"

　"你要恋爱就必须要谈"

音乐一响

你就得上场了。

不管你是否已记熟了

四个环节,你上了场你就得使用

第一个道具。

For Joe Hisaishi

Is it possible that a flame

is black?

It burns or climbs up

from inside the body to the top

it knows nothing about panic

it is reserved like a conductor

who directs music

after it learned to panic

it started to rush outwards

it leads the band to rush outwards

to rush outwards like a swarm of bees

when it rushes outwards like a swarm of bees

it runs into

a crazily-burning

white flame

致久石让

有没有一包火焰

是黑色的?

它从身体的内部

往上烧或者说往上爬

它不知道恐慌

它矜持得如同一个指挥家

指挥着音乐

而它知道恐慌的时候

它开始往外跑

它带着乐队往外跑

一窝蜂往外跑

而就这样一窝蜂往外跑的时候

它偏偏跑进了

疯狂燃烧着的

白色的火焰

One is Still in Sweden, The Other One is Already in Norway

One person

becomes dizzy

after he flies

The other one

wants to fly more

after he flies

If these two persons fly together

when one is still in Sweden

the other one is already

in Norway

With a bundle of light

roll you away

with a bundle of light

take you away

with a bundle of light

pull you away

with a bundle of light

grasp your desire tight

We often saw

half woman

the smile is half

the plumpness is half

the nude is half

the thought is half

The spider

crawling down the glass

the spiderman

crawling down the glass

both are transparent

like drops of liquid

Cry it out

cry with your eyes

cry with your mouth

cry with your tongue

finally go cry with your nose

On paper

you can read about clothes

on clothes

you can read words about paper

Only by getting close to a sailor

can you get closer to Europe

Only by getting close to Siren

can you get closer to Europe

Only by getting close to Heaven

can you get closer to Europe

Only by getting close to death

can you get closer to Europe

一个还在瑞典,一个已到挪威

一个人

飞了

他就晕

另一个人

飞了

还想飞

如果两个人

一起飞

一个还在瑞典

一个已到

挪威

用一束光

把你卷走

用一束光

把你带走

用一束光

把你拉走

用一束光

攥紧你的欲望

我们经常看到

半截的女人

微笑是半截

丰满是半截

裸体是半截

想法是半截

从玻璃上

爬下的蜘蛛

从玻璃上

爬上的蜘蛛人

都透明得

像一滴滴液体

哭吧

哭你的眼睛

哭你的嘴巴

哭你的舌头

最后才哭你的鼻子

在纸上

你能读到衣服

在衣服上

你能读到纸的文字

靠近水手时

　才更靠近欧洲

靠近海妖时

　才更靠近欧洲

靠近天堂时

　才更靠近欧洲

靠近死亡时

　才更靠近欧洲

Passing Through These Things, Enough Movement

We've all come here riding horses.

One horse. Two horses. Three horses. Four horses. Five horses. Six horses.

In the sky dark clouds press down.

Between the dark clouds and far mountains is drawn a white line.

Just one white horse.

Just her.

Just her eye.

Just her eyes.

Just her eyes shed.

Just her eyes shedding.

Just her eyes shedding tears.

Just her eyes are shedding teardrops.

通过这些事物,足够地移动

我们都是骑着马来的。

一匹。二匹。三匹。四匹。五匹。六匹。

天上压着乌云。

乌云与远山间勾画着白线。

只有一匹白马。

只有它的。

只有它的眼。

只有它的眼睛。

只有它的眼睛流。

只有它的眼睛流着。

只有它的眼睛流着眼。

只有它的眼睛流着眼泪。

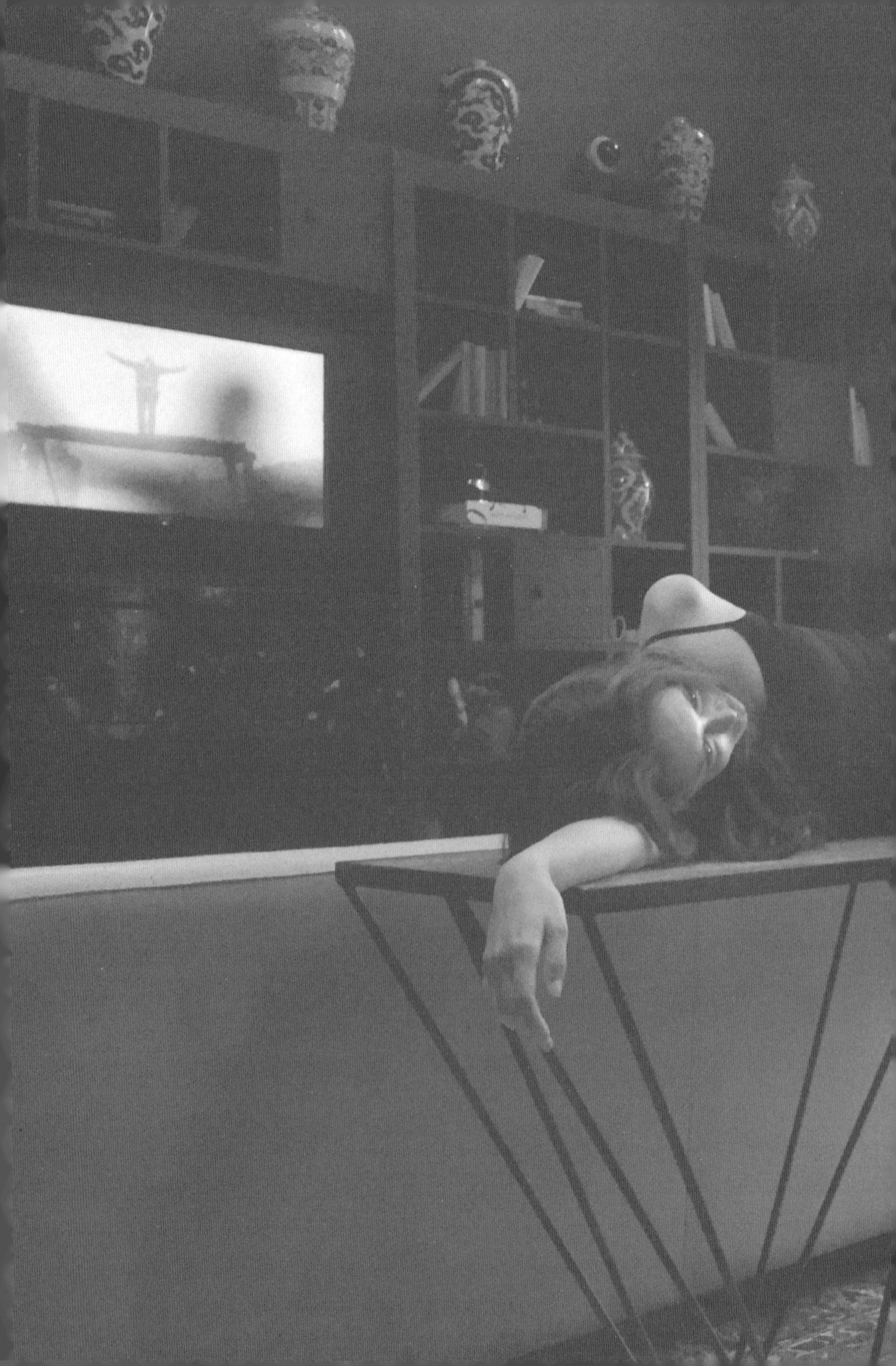

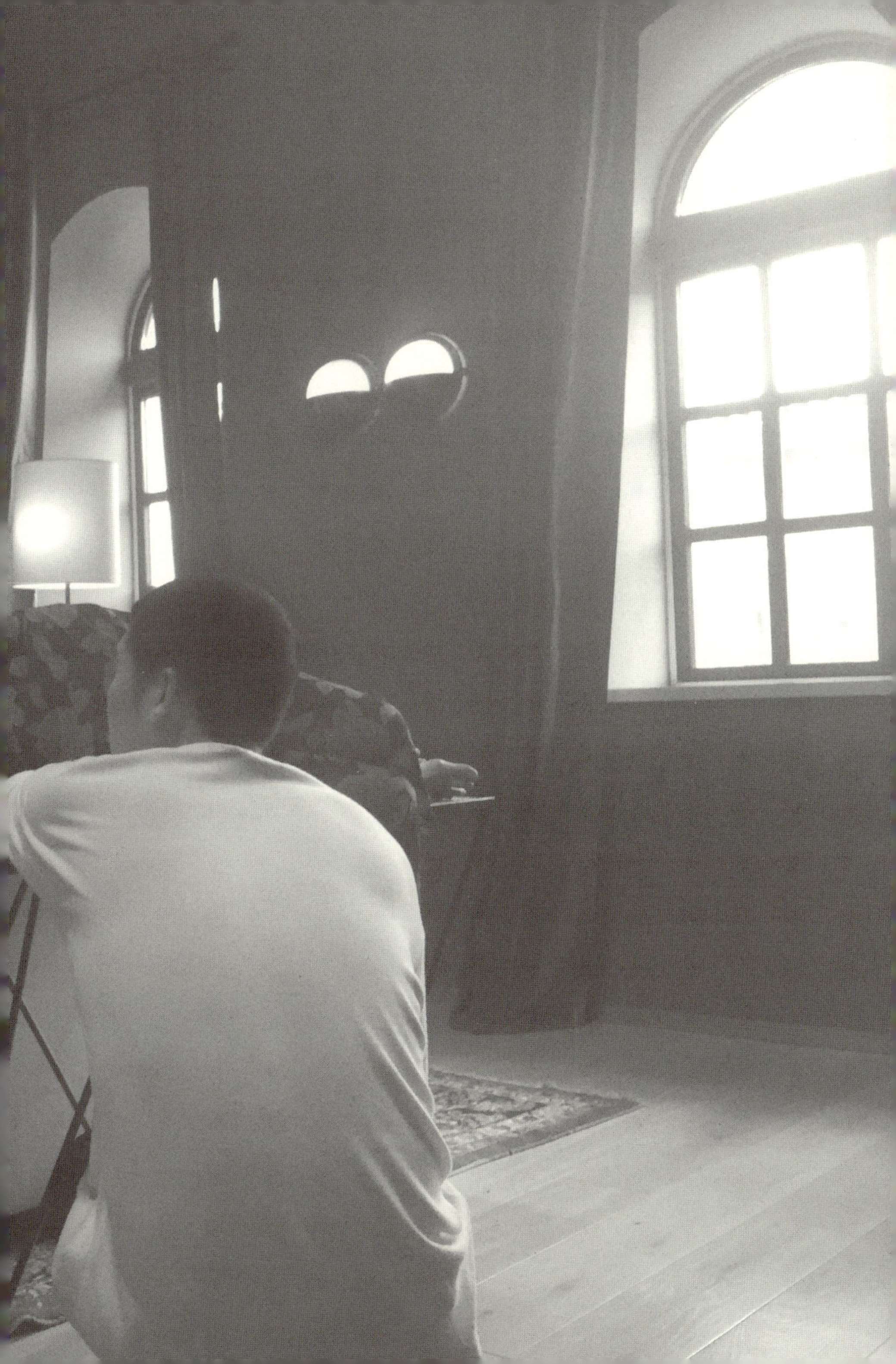

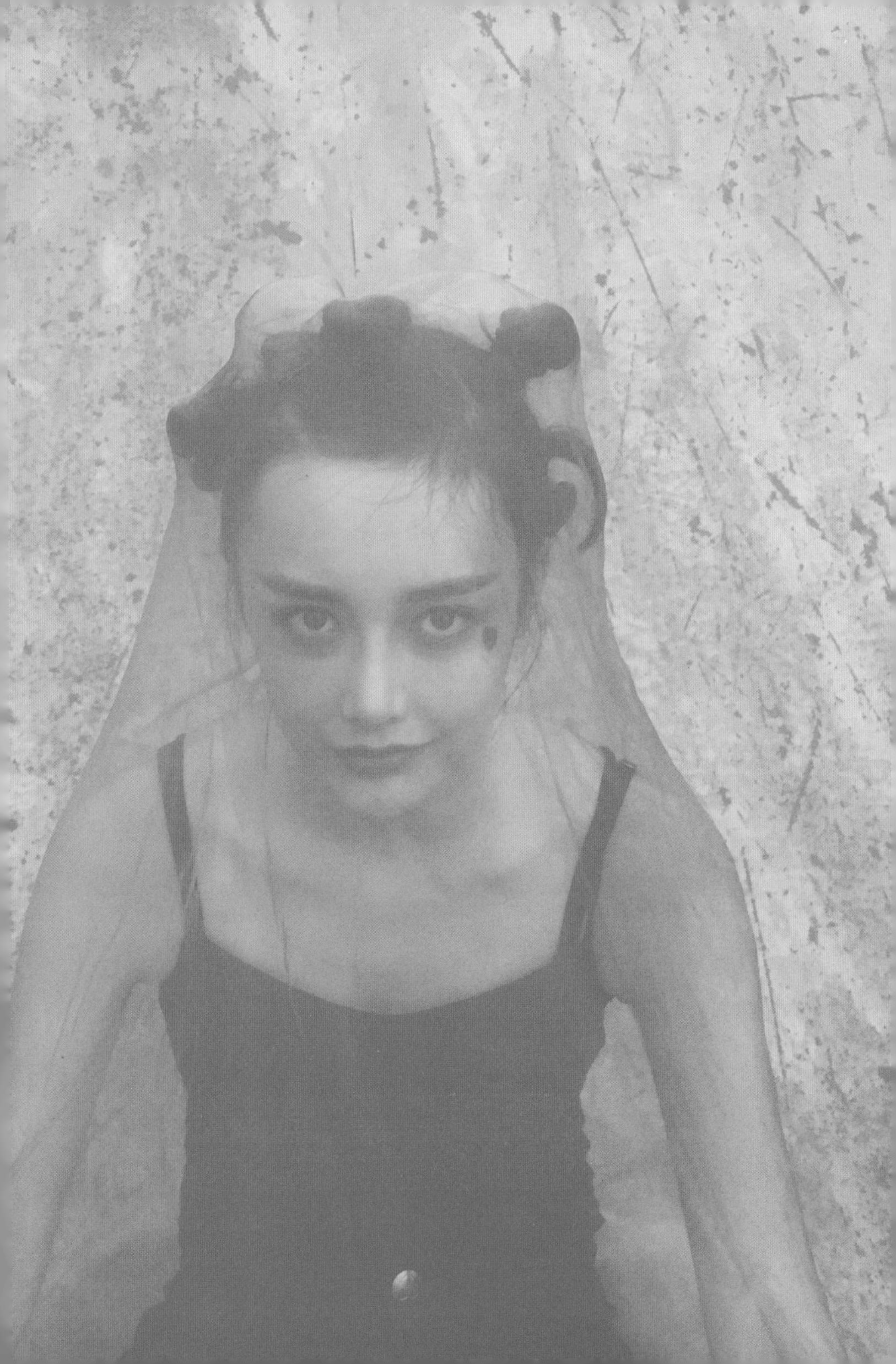

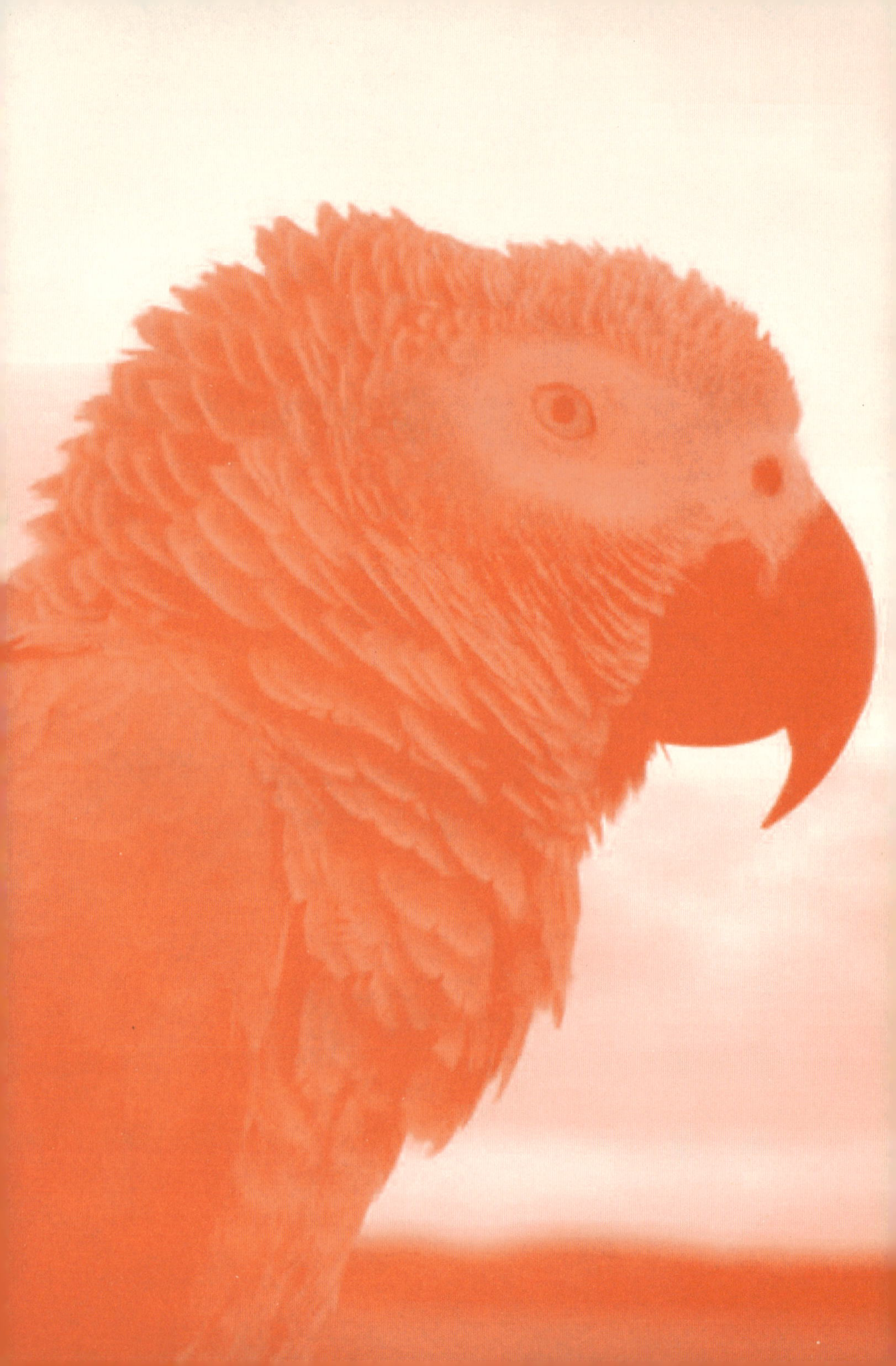

If The Wheat Dies

286

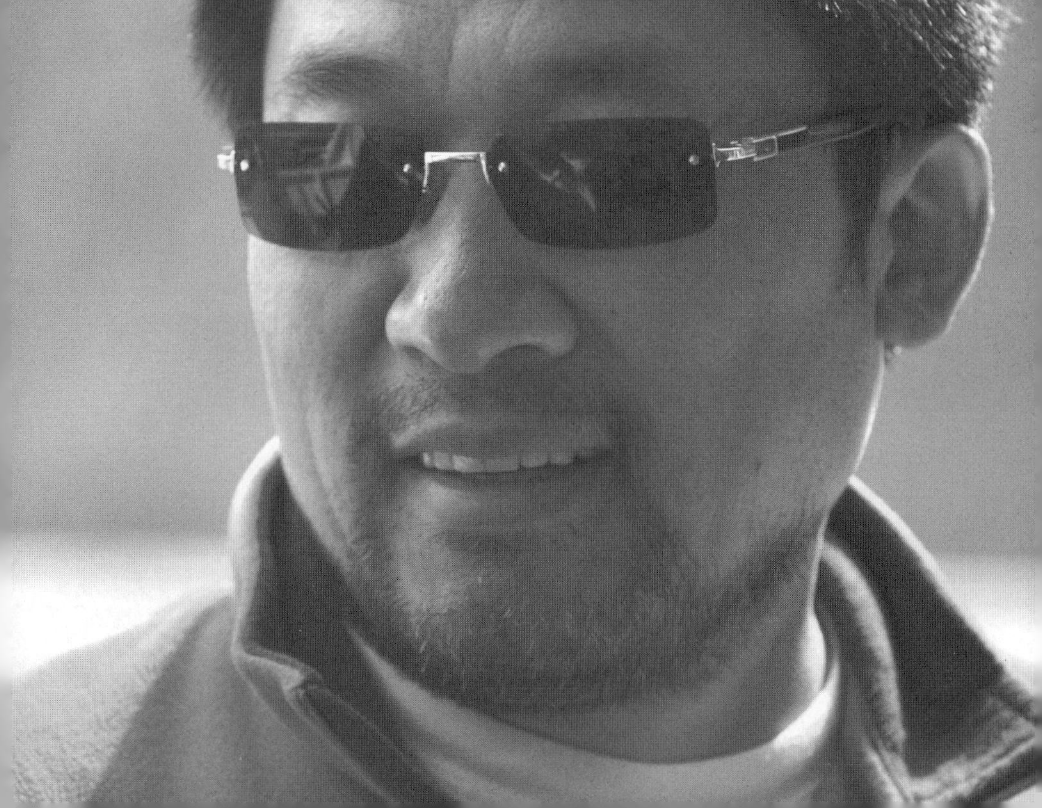

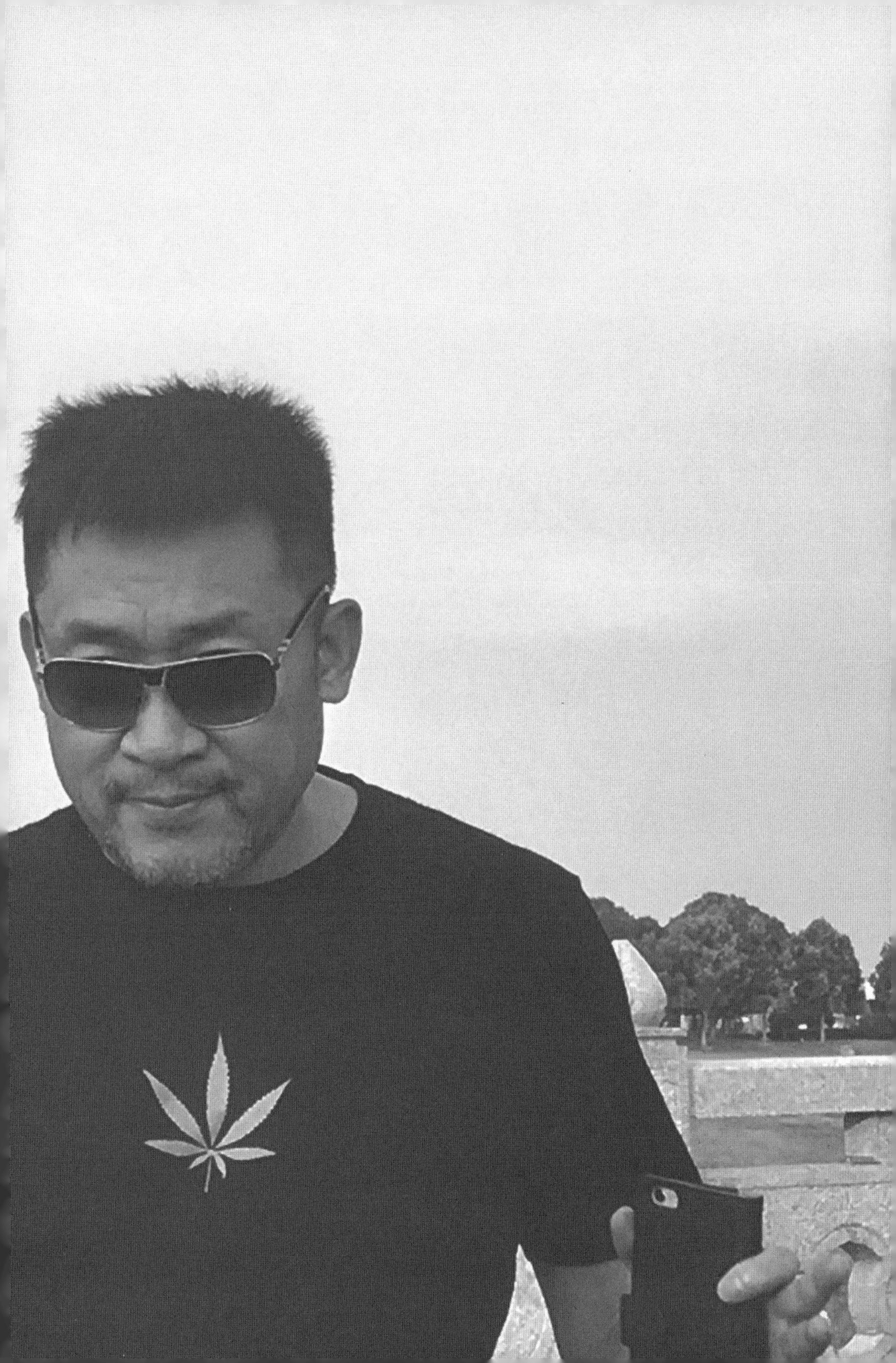

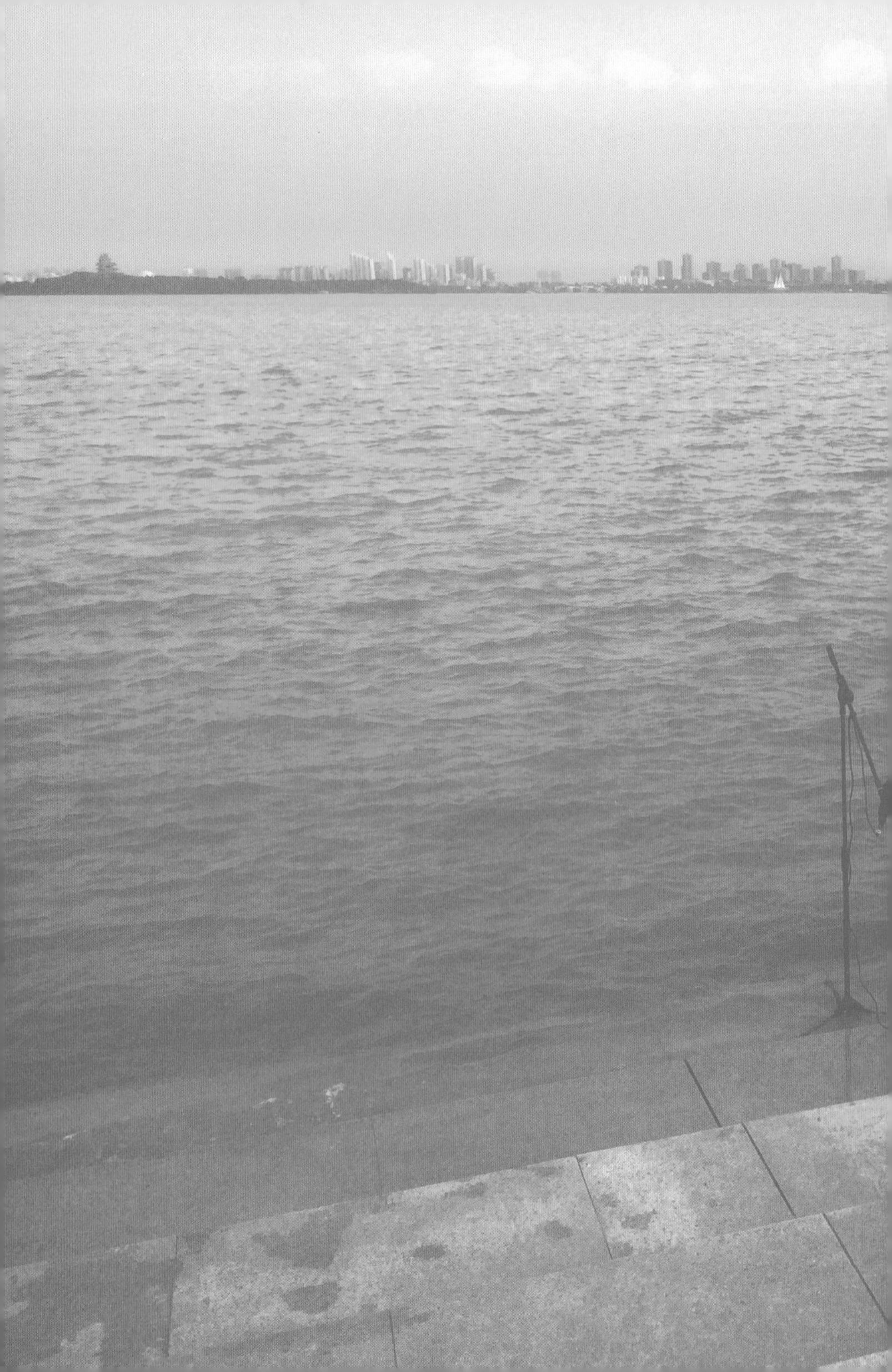

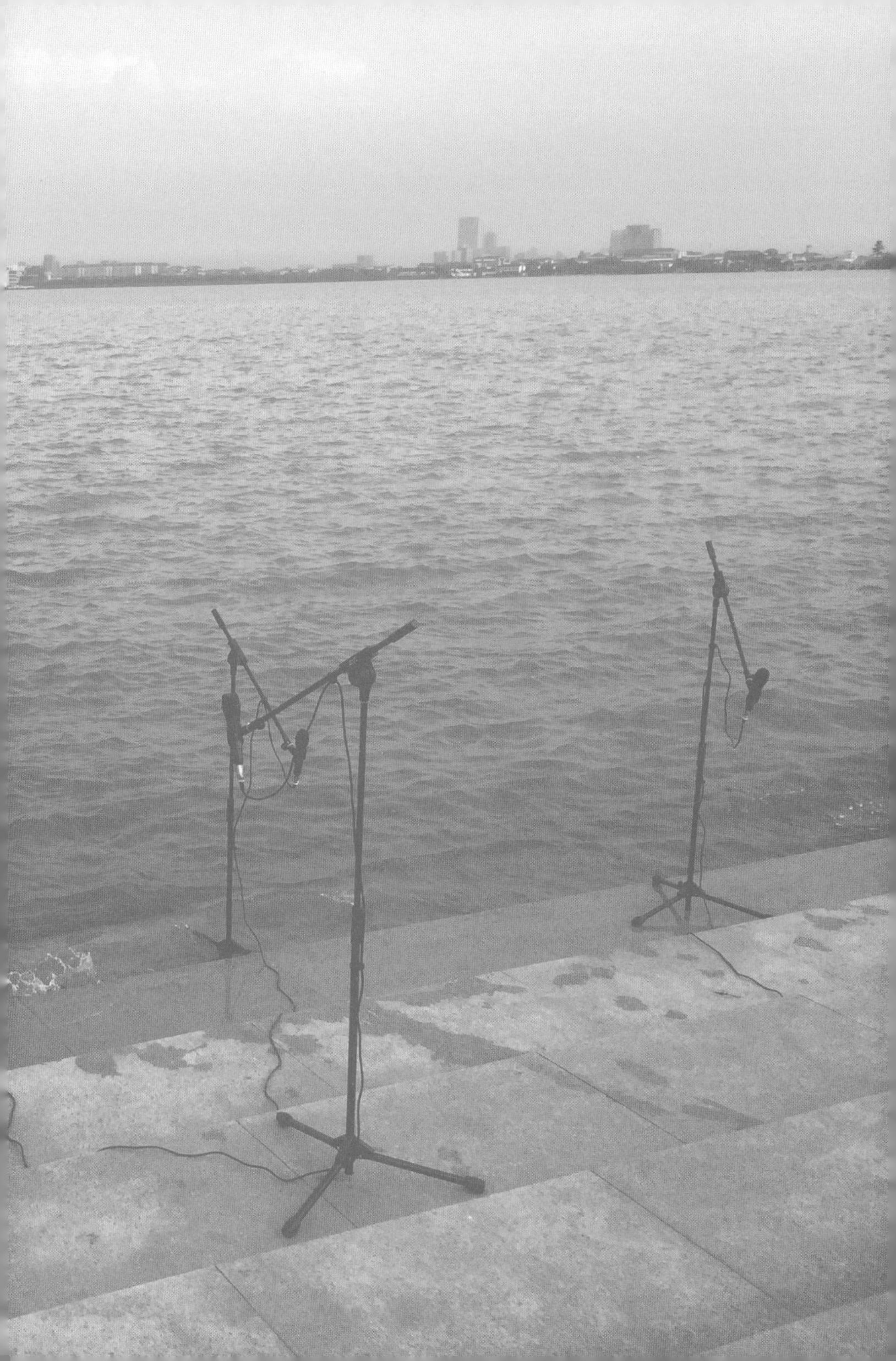

图书在版编目（CIP）数据

如果麦子死了 = If the Wheat Dies : 汉英对照 / 周亚平著 ; 郑秀才，（美）杰弗里（Jeffrey Twitchell-Waas），（美）魏朴（Paul Manfredi）译. —— 南京 : 江苏凤凰文艺出版社，2021.5
ISBN 978-7-5594-5509-3

Ⅰ. ①如… Ⅱ. ①周… ②郑… ③杰… ④魏… Ⅲ. ①诗集－中国－当代－汉、英 Ⅳ. ① I227

中国版本图书馆CIP数据核字（2020）第259113号

If the Wheat Dies 如果麦子死了

周亚平　著

郑秀才　Jeffrey Twitchell-Waas　Paul Manfredi　译

出 版 人	张在健
选题策划	于奎潮
责任编辑	王娱瑶　徐　辰
责任印制	刘　巍
出版发行	江苏凤凰文艺出版社
	南京市中央路165号，邮编：210009
出版社网址	http://www.jswenyi.com
印　　刷	苏州越洋印刷有限公司
开　　本	880×1230 毫米　1/32
印　　张	9.5
字　　数	120千字
版　　次	2021年5月第1版　2021年5月第1次印刷
标准书号	ISBN　978-7-5594-5509-3
定　　价	128.00元

江苏凤凰文艺版图书凡印刷、装订错误，可向出版社调换，联系电话 025-83280257

出 品 人_张在健
选题策划_于奉翰
责任编辑_王蜜瑶　　　书 名
书籍设计_马海之
媒体联系_刘 畅　　025-83280238
销售联系_刘承北　　025-83208579
官网网址_www.jsweny1.com